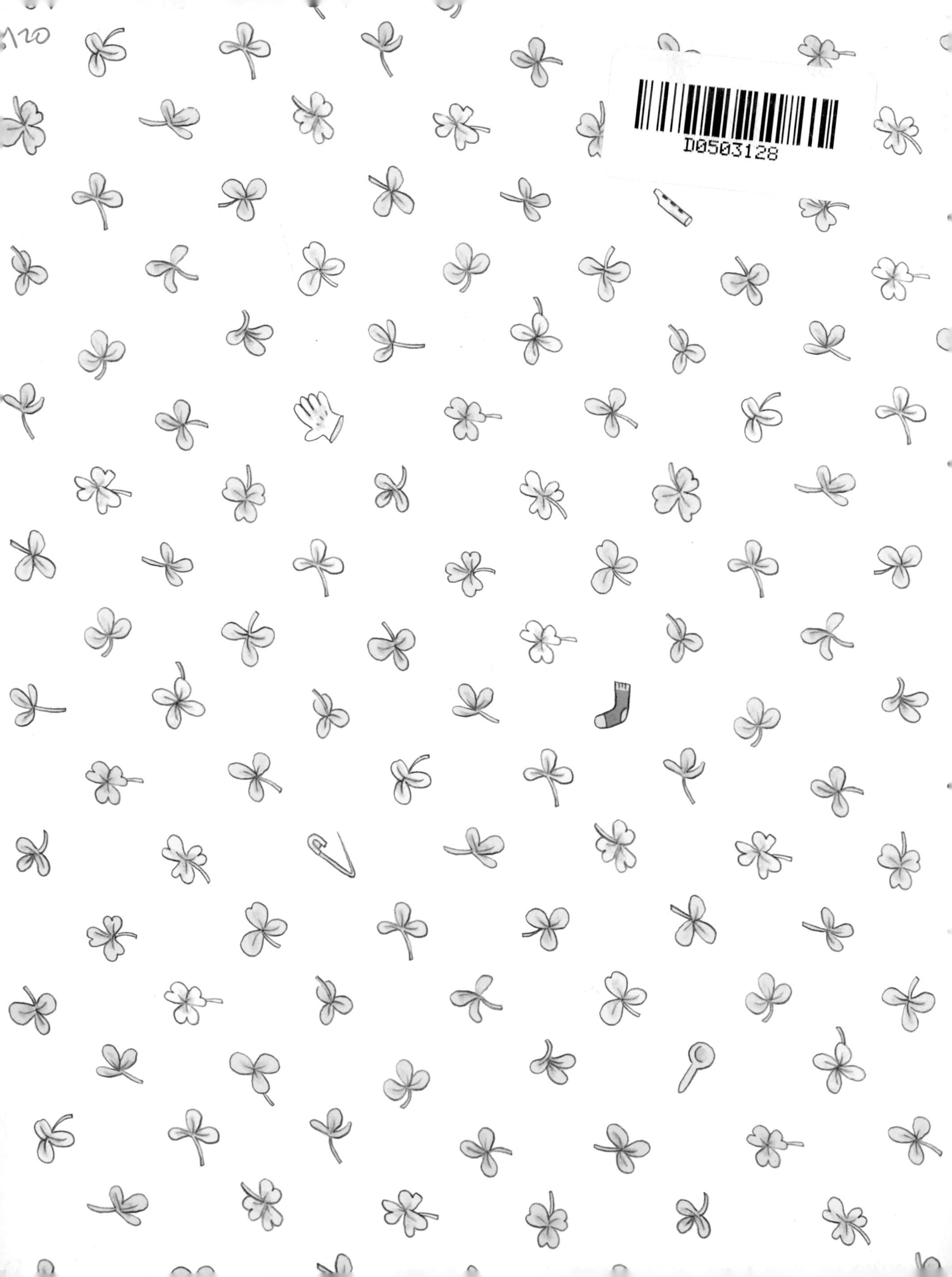

For Émilie, an eminent specialist in mole snouts and a remarkable misplacer of things — Cathon

First edition 2018
Published with the permission of Comme des géants inc.,
38, rue Sainte-Anne, Varennes, Quebec, Canada J3X 1R5
All rights reserved.
Translation rights arranged through the VeroK Agency, Barcelona, Spain

Published in English in 2019 by Owlkids Books Inc.
Translation © 2019 Susan Ouriou
Published in French under the title *Mimose et Sam : À la recherche des lunettes roses*

Owlkids Books acknowledges the financial support of the Canada Council for the Arts, the Ontario Arts Council, the Government of Canada through the Canada Book Fund (CBF), and the Government of Ontario through the Ontario Creates Book Initiative for our publishing activities.

Published in Canada by
Owlkids Books Inc.
1 Eglinton Avenue East
Toronto, ON M4P 3A1

Published in the United States by
Owlkids Books Inc.
1700 Fourth Street
Berkeley, CA 94710

Library and Archives Canada Cataloguing in Publication

Cathon, 1990-
[Mimose et Sam, à la recherche des lunettes roses. English]
    Poppy and Sam and the mole mystery / by Cathon ; translated by Susan Ouriou.

Translation of: Mimose et Sam, à la recherche des lunettes roses.
ISBN 978-1-77147-379-8 (hardcover)

    I. Ouriou, Susan, translator II. Title. III. Title: Mole mystery.
IV. Title: Mimose et Sam, à la recherche des lunettes roses. English.

PS8605.A8786M5513 2019   jC843'.6   C2018-906584-2

Library of Congress Control Number: 2018963963

 ONTARIO ARTS COUNCIL
CONSEIL DES ARTS DE L'ONTARIO
an Ontario government agency
un organisme du gouvernement de l'Ontario

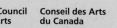 Canada Council
for the Arts

Conseil des Arts
du Canada

 Canada

Manufactured in Shenzhen, Guangdong, China, in February 2019, by WKT Co. Ltd.
Job #18CB3236

A   B   C   D   E   F

 Publisher of Chirp, Chickadee and OWL
www.owlkidsbooks.com

Owlkids Books is a division of
 bayard canada

POPPY & SAM
AND THE MOLE MYSTERY

By CATHON

Translated by Susan Ouriou

Owlkids Books

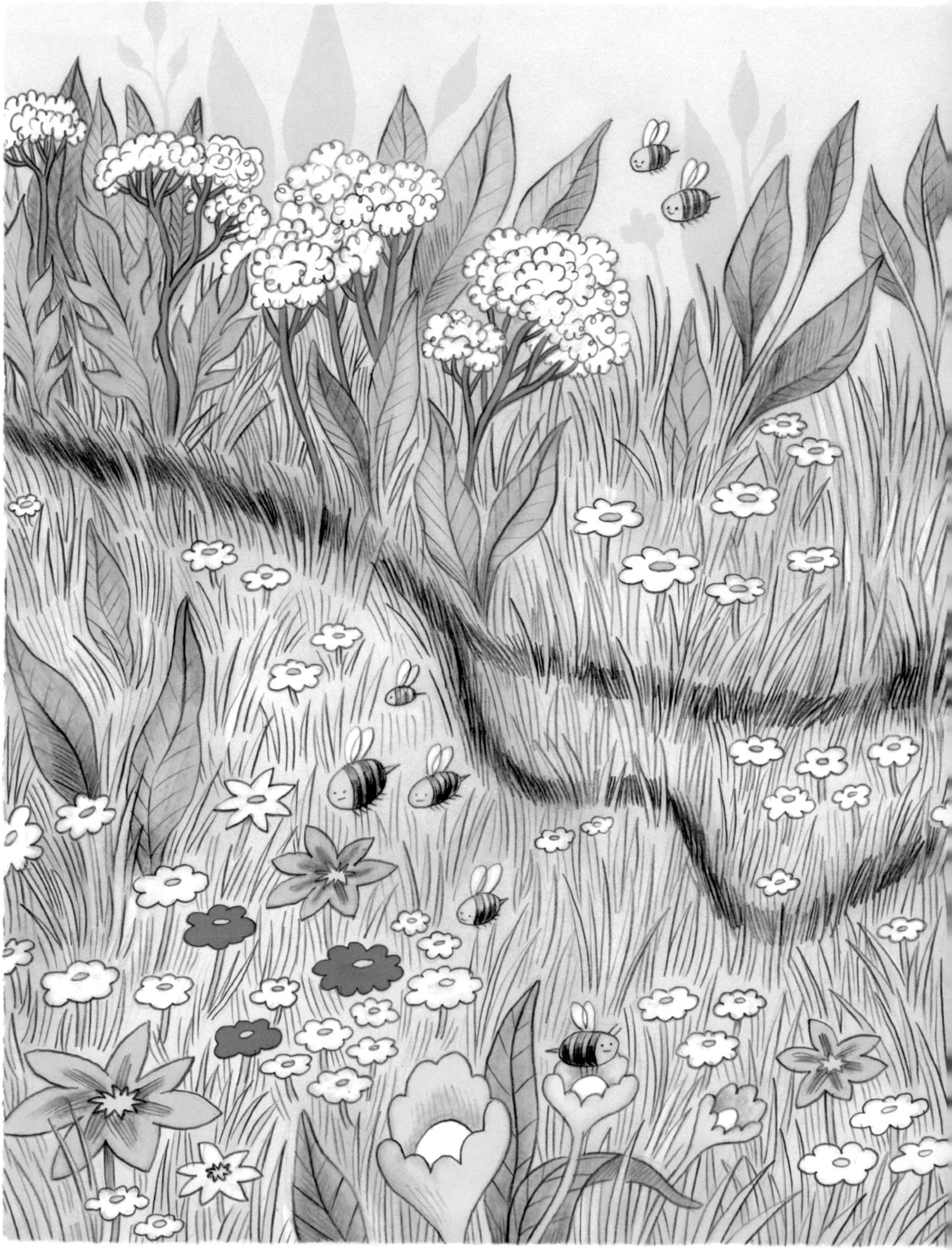

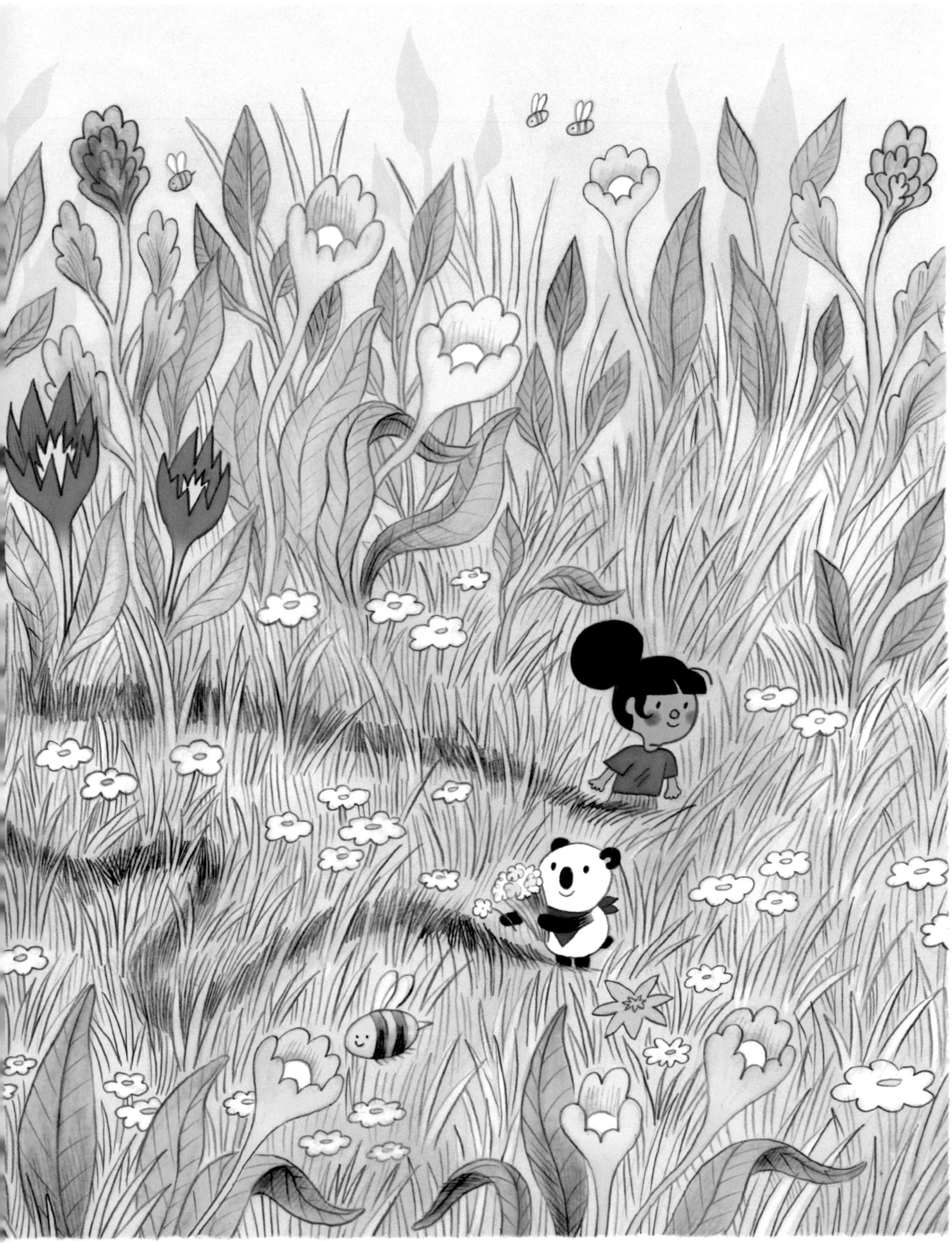

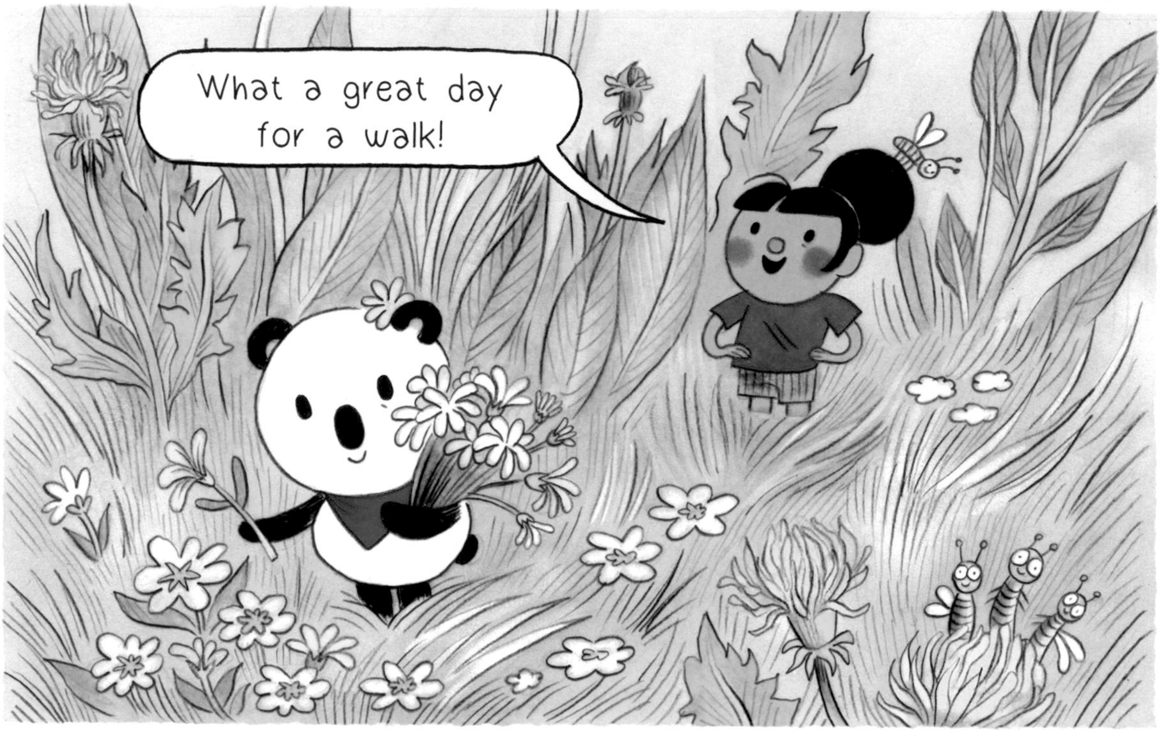
What a great day for a walk!

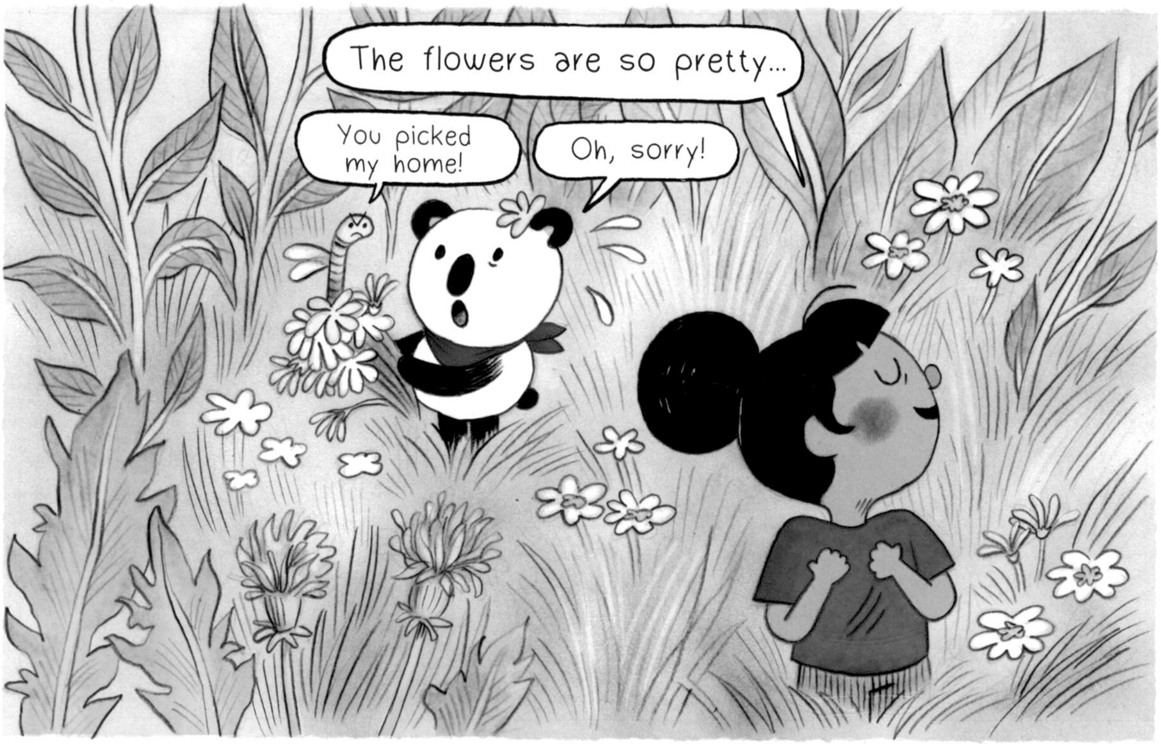
The flowers are so pretty...
You picked my home!
Oh, sorry!

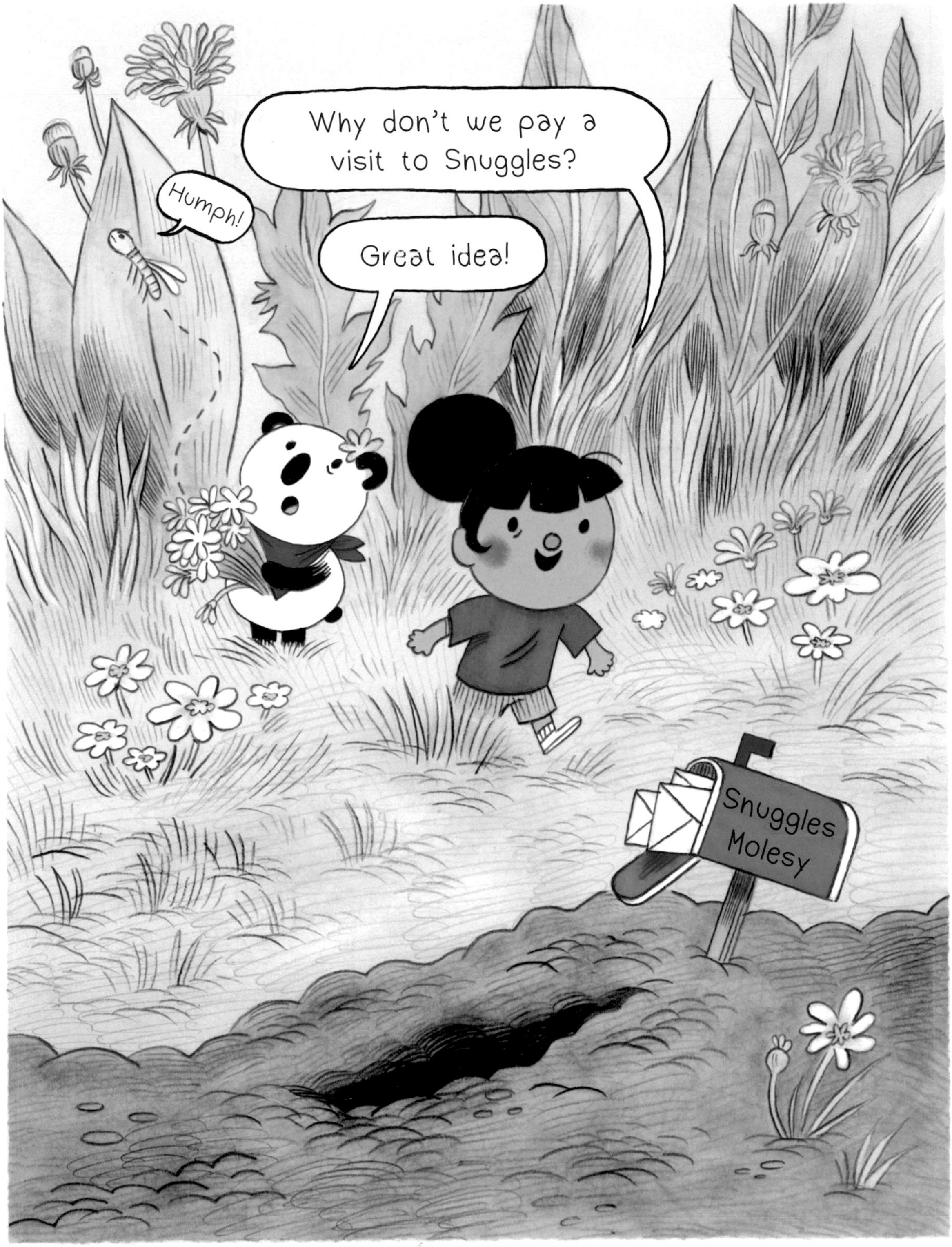

Why don't we pay a visit to Snuggles?
Humph!
Great idea!
Snuggles Molesy

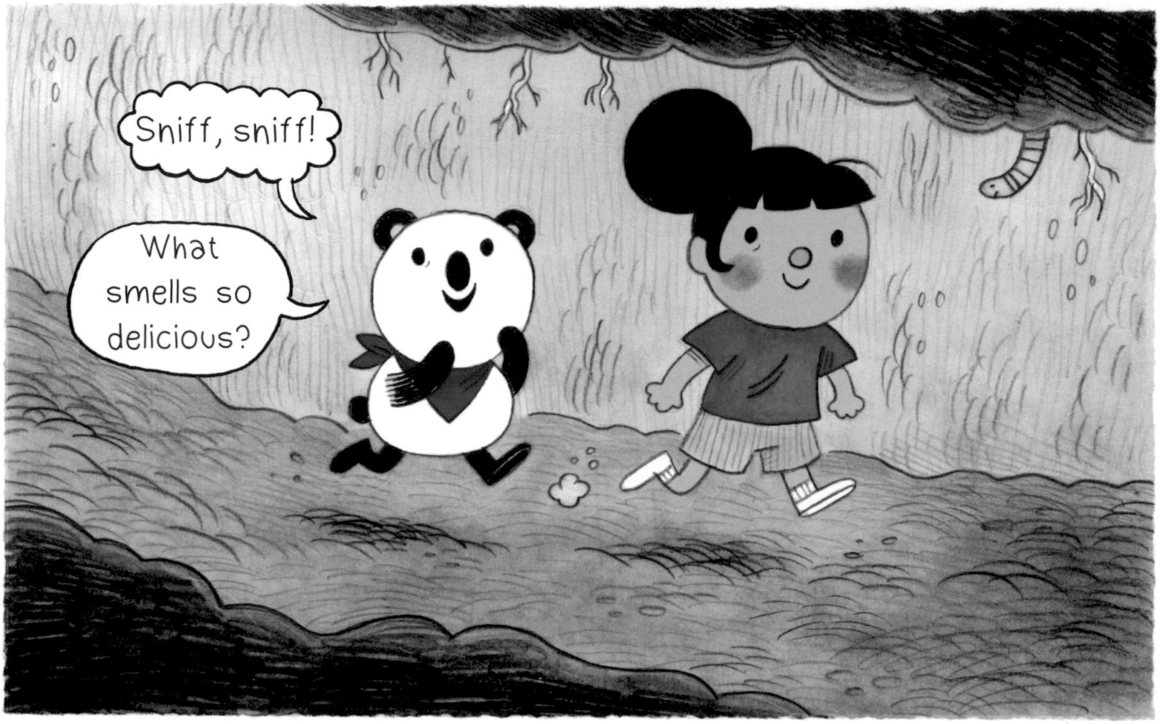
Sniff, sniff!
What smells so delicious?

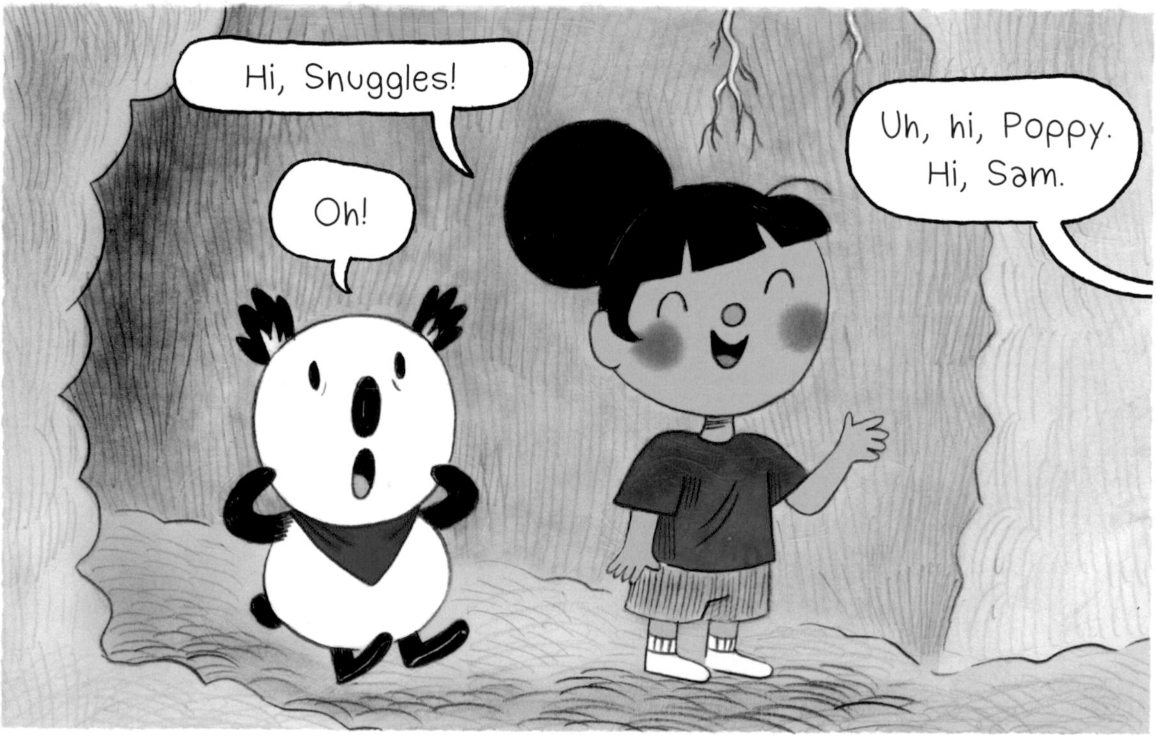
Hi, Snuggles!
Oh!
Uh, hi, Poppy. Hi, Sam.

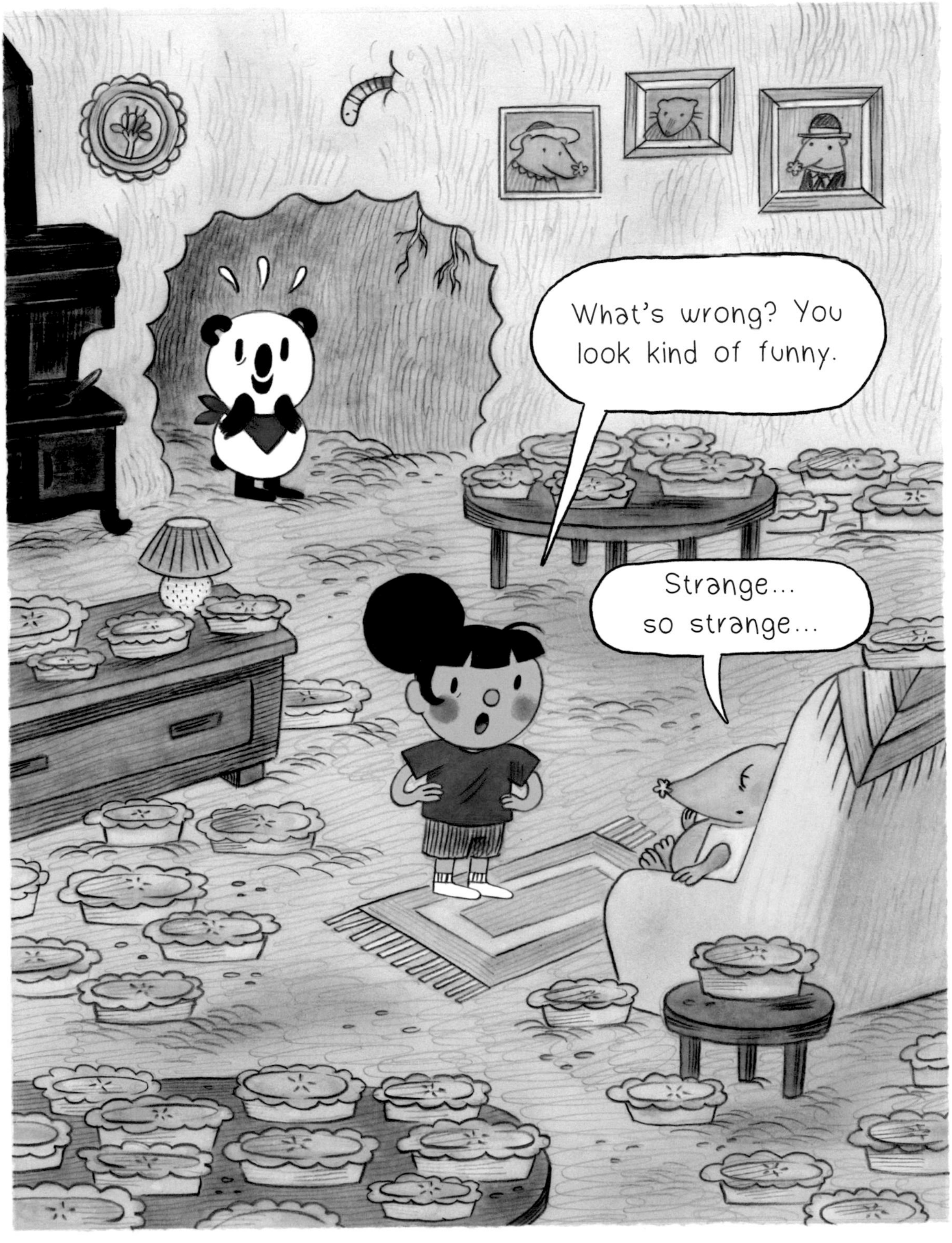
What's wrong? You look kind of funny.
Strange... so strange...

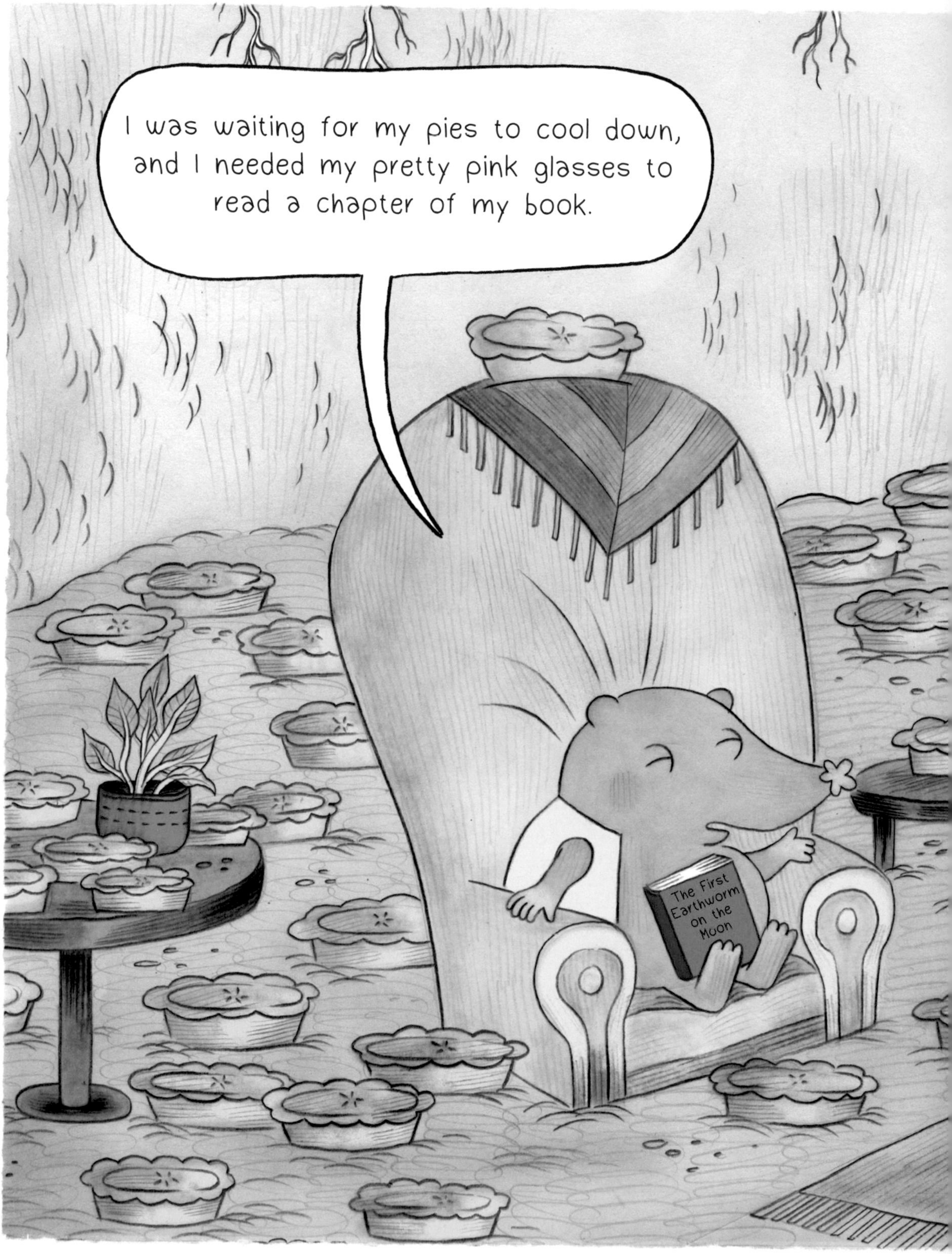
I was waiting for my pies to cool down, and I needed my pretty pink glasses to read a chapter of my book.
The First Earthworm on the Moon

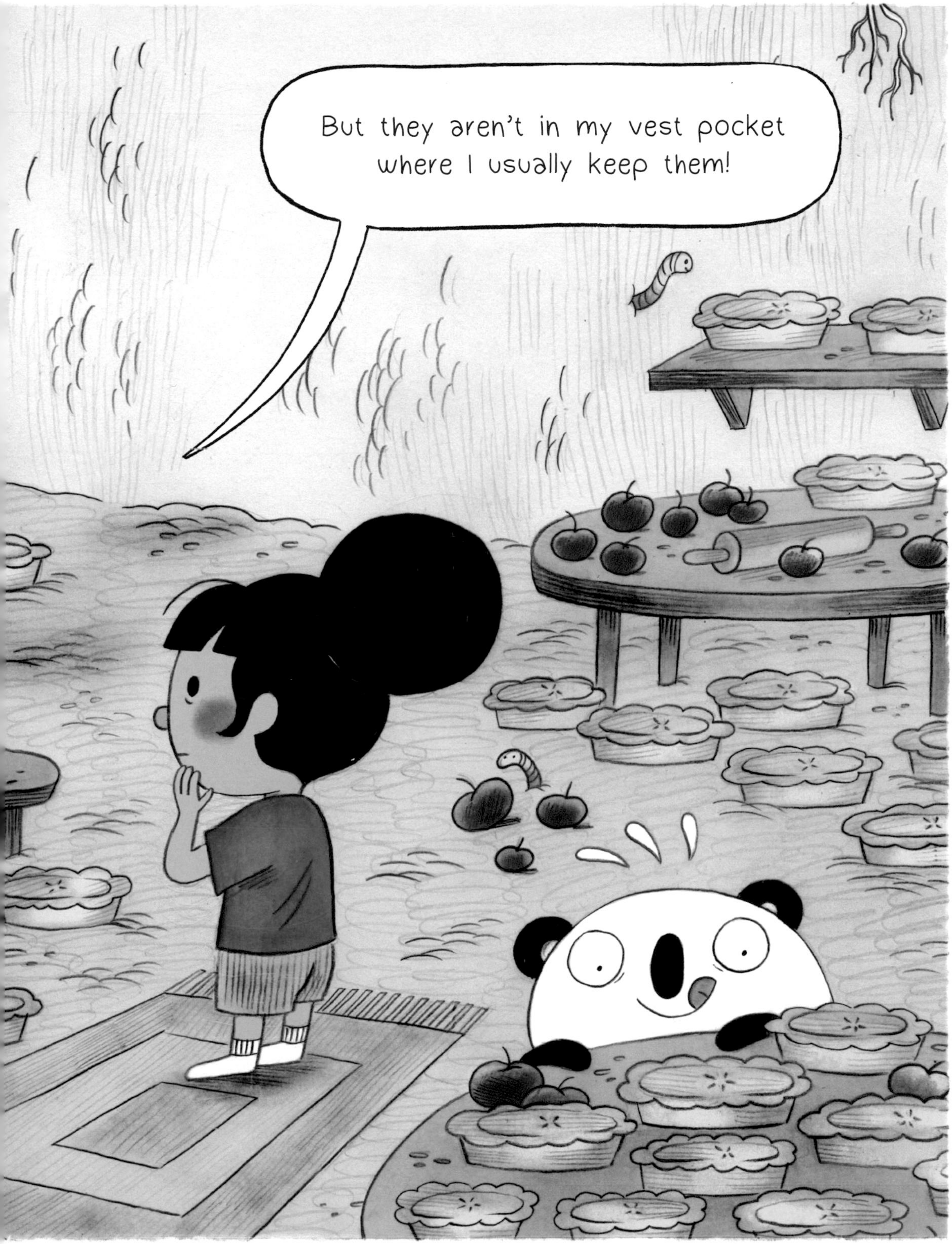
But they aren't in my vest pocket where I usually keep them!

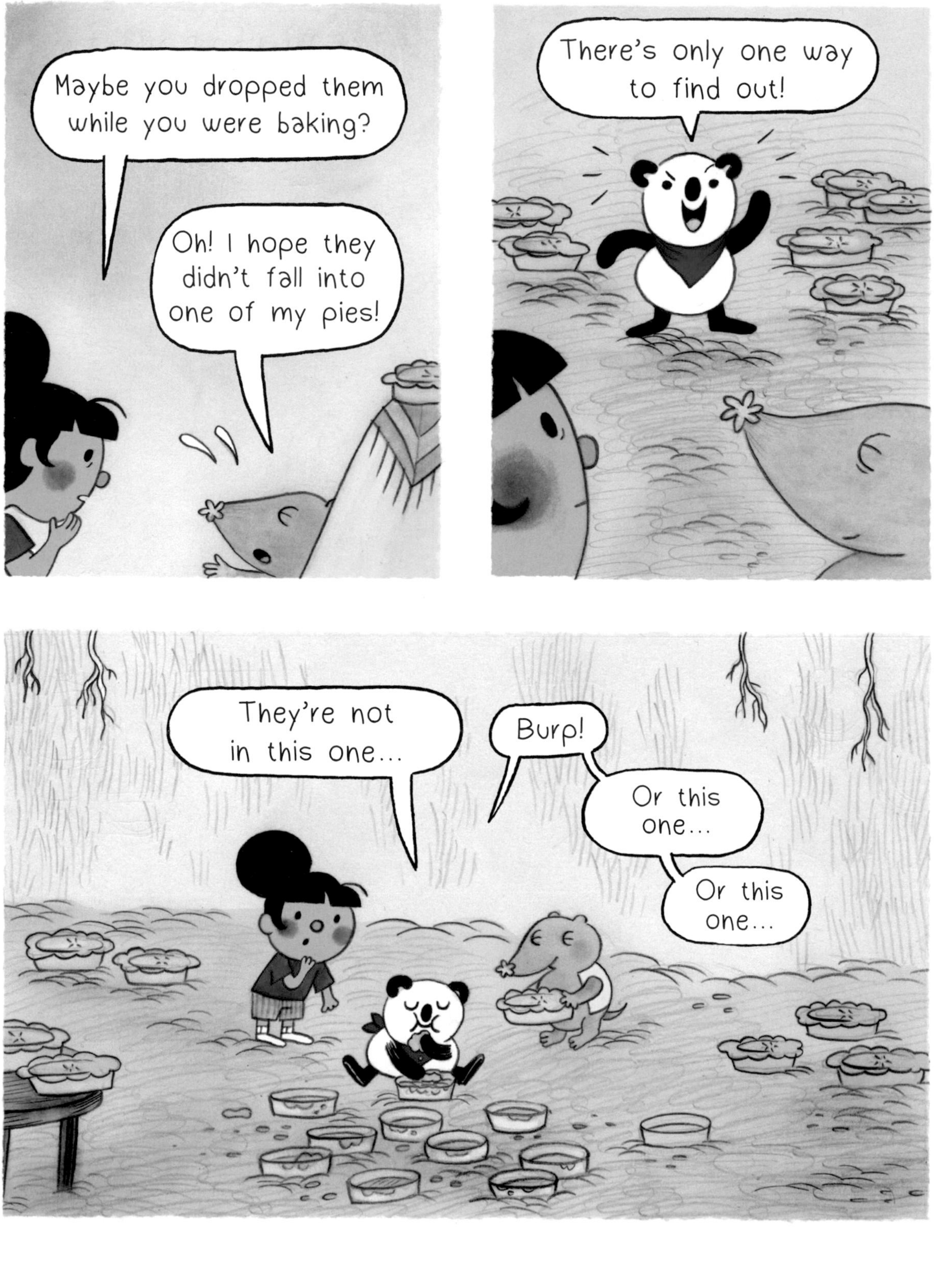
Maybe you dropped them while you were baking?
Oh! I hope they didn't fall into one of my pies!
There's only one way to find out!
They're not in this one...
Burp!
Or this one...
Or this one...

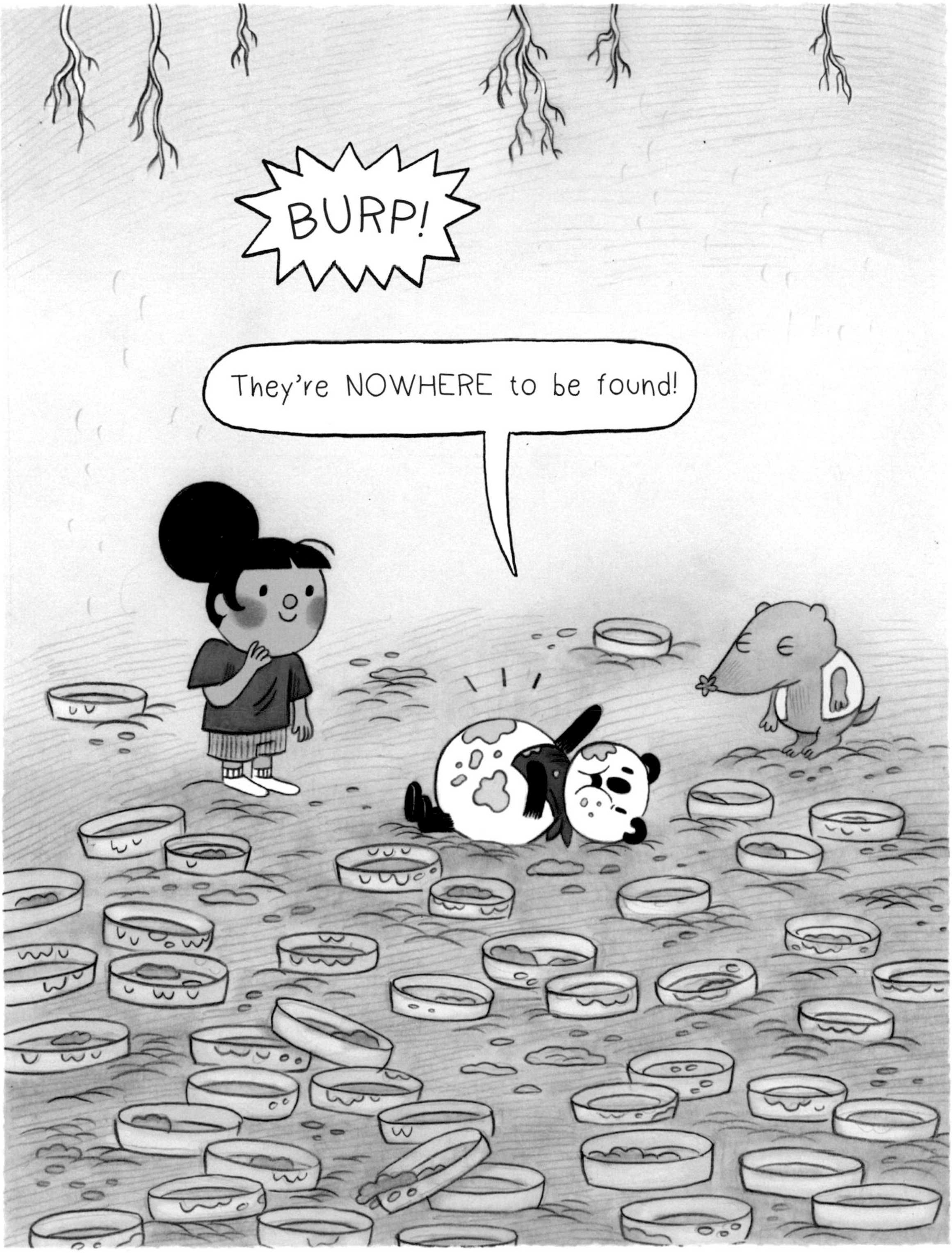
BURP!
They're NOWHERE to be found!

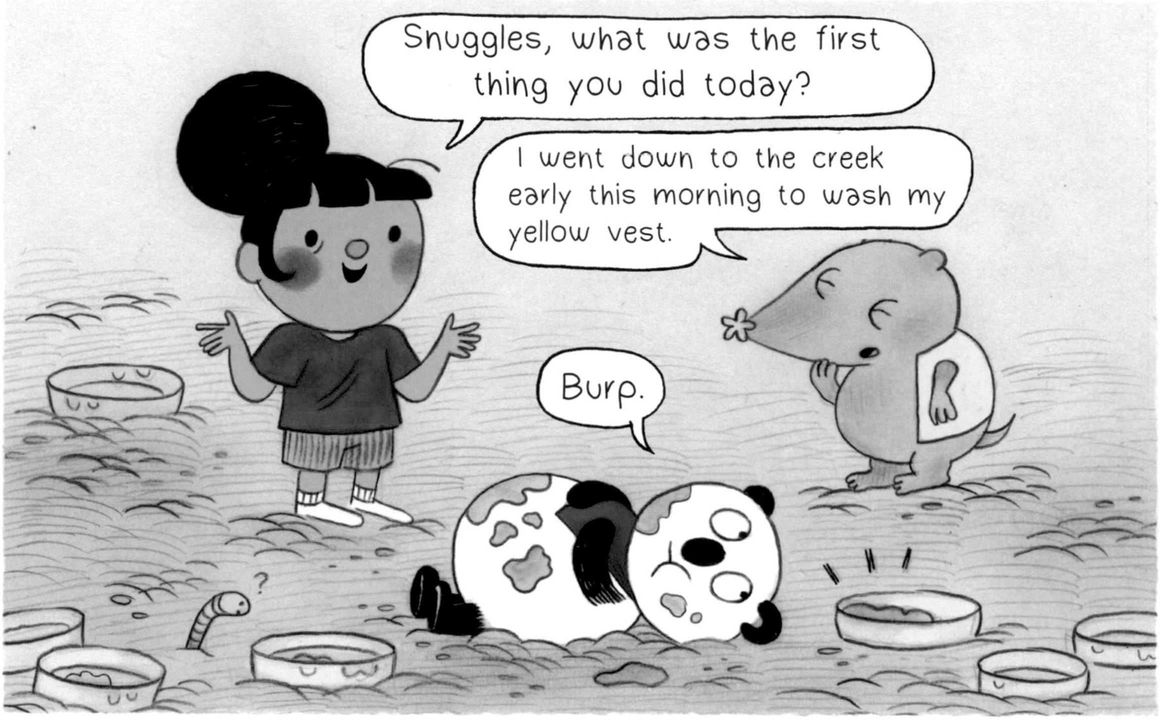
Snuggles, what was the first thing you did today?
I went down to the creek early this morning to wash my yellow vest.
Burp.

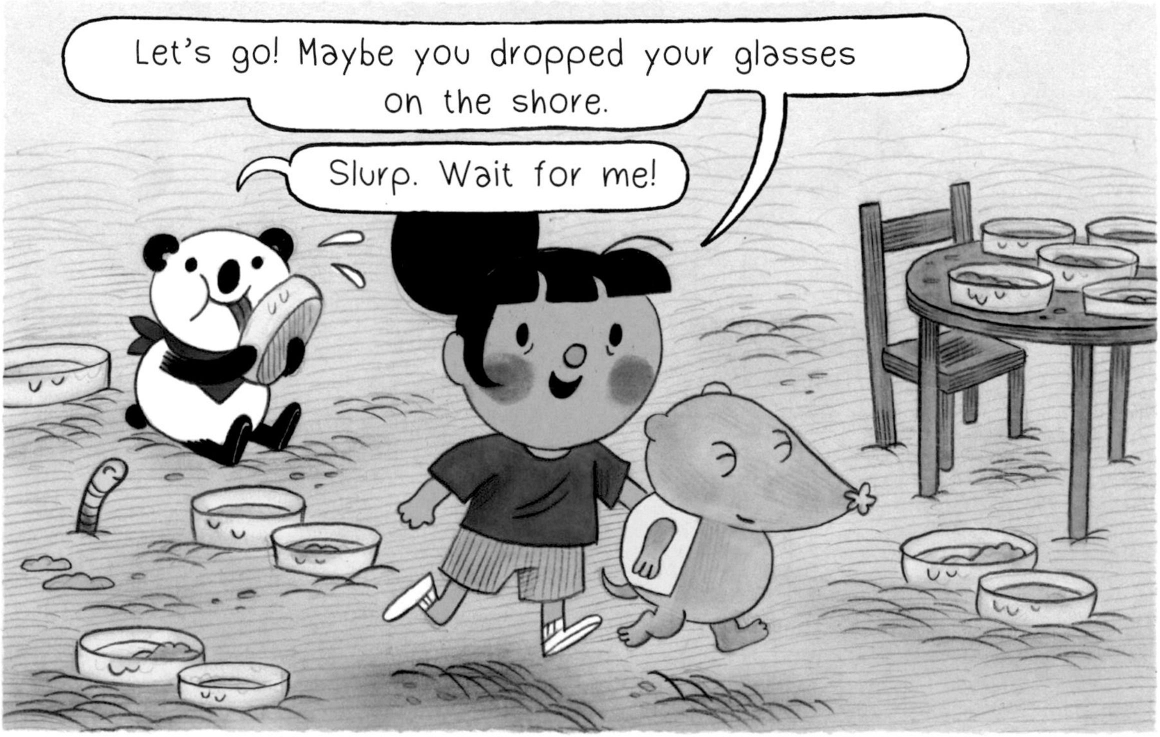
Let's go! Maybe you dropped your glasses on the shore.
Slurp. Wait for me!

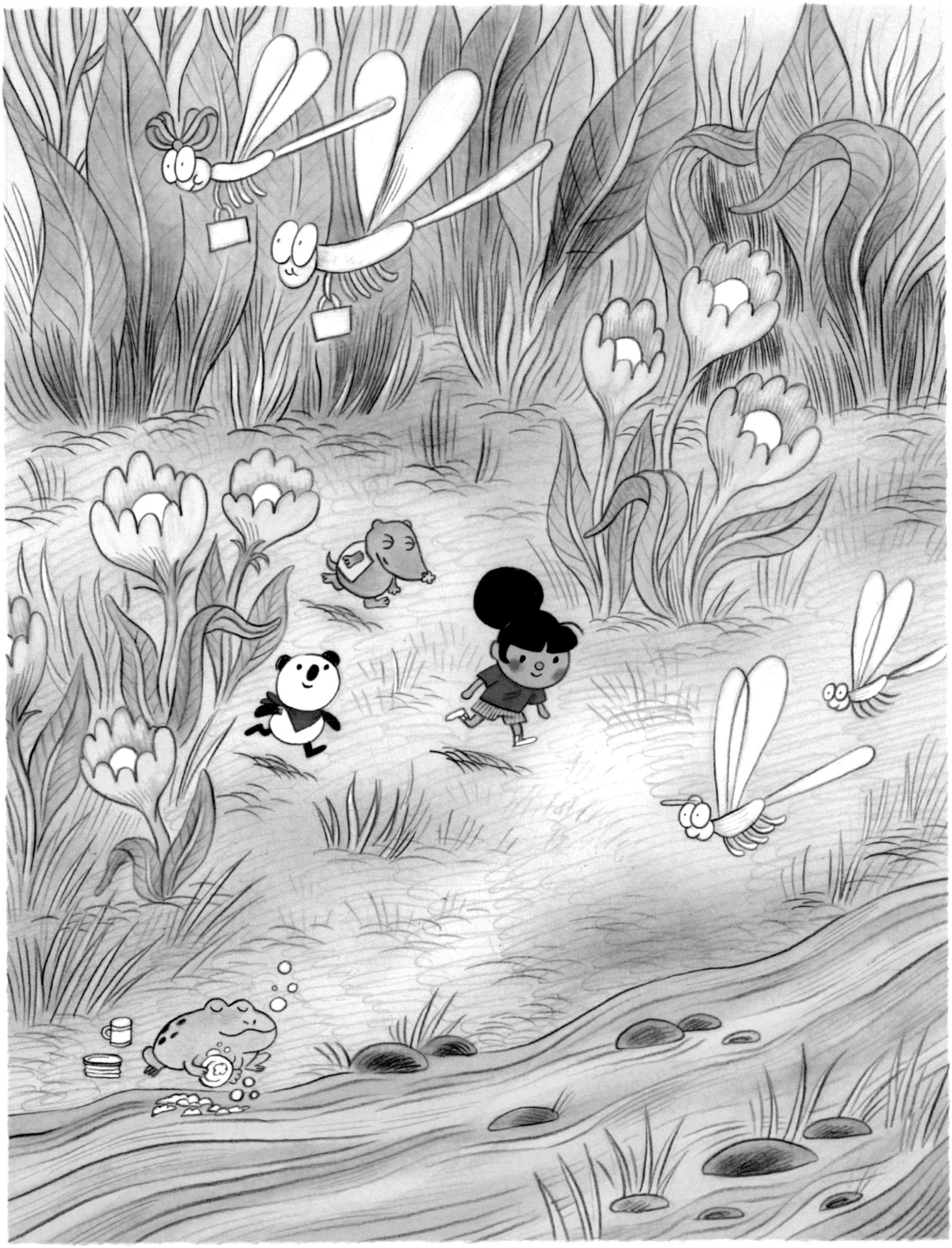

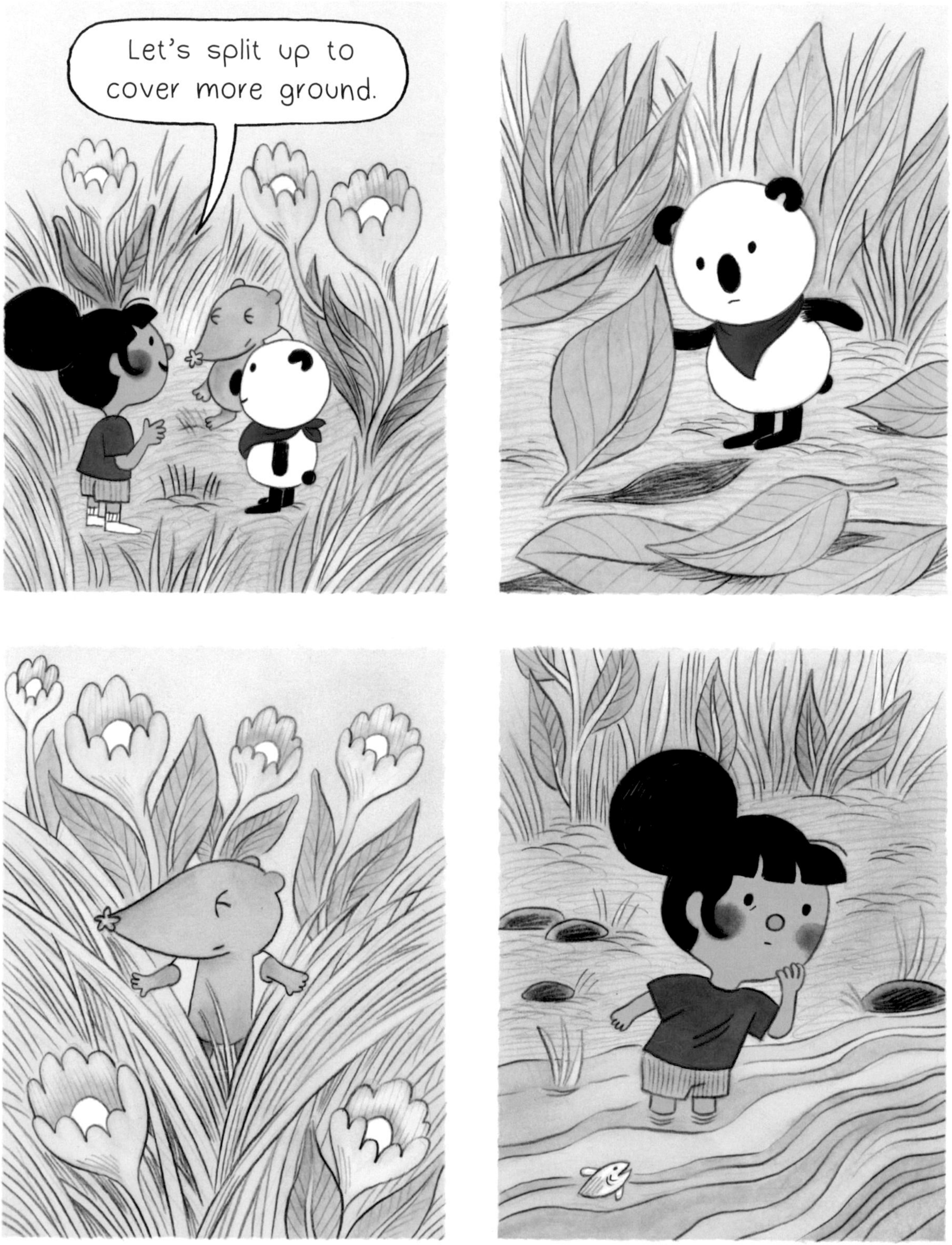
Let's split up to cover more ground.

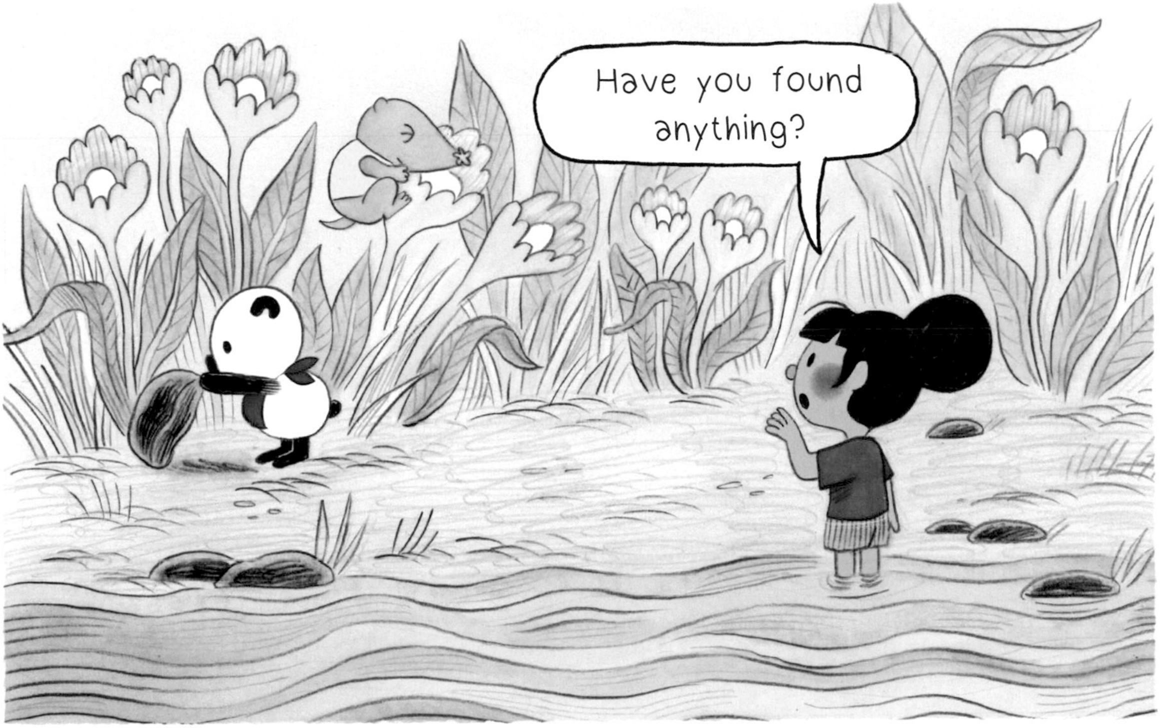
Have you found anything?

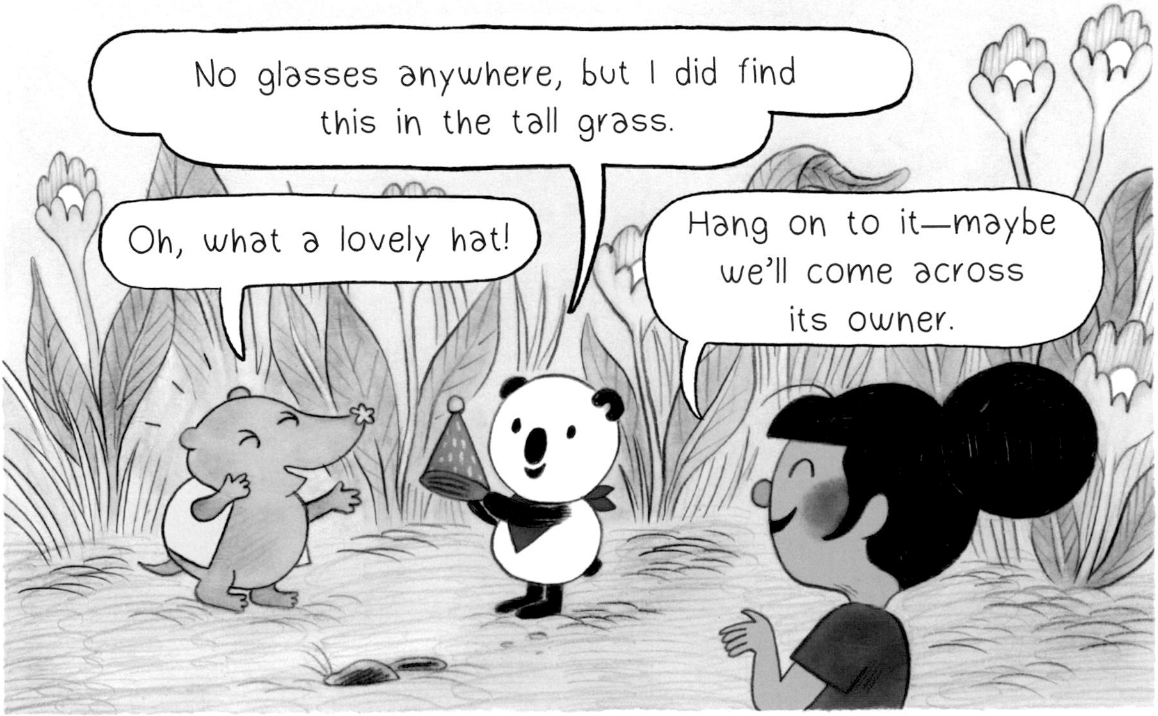
No glasses anywhere, but I did find this in the tall grass.
Oh, what a lovely hat!
Hang on to it—maybe we'll come across its owner.

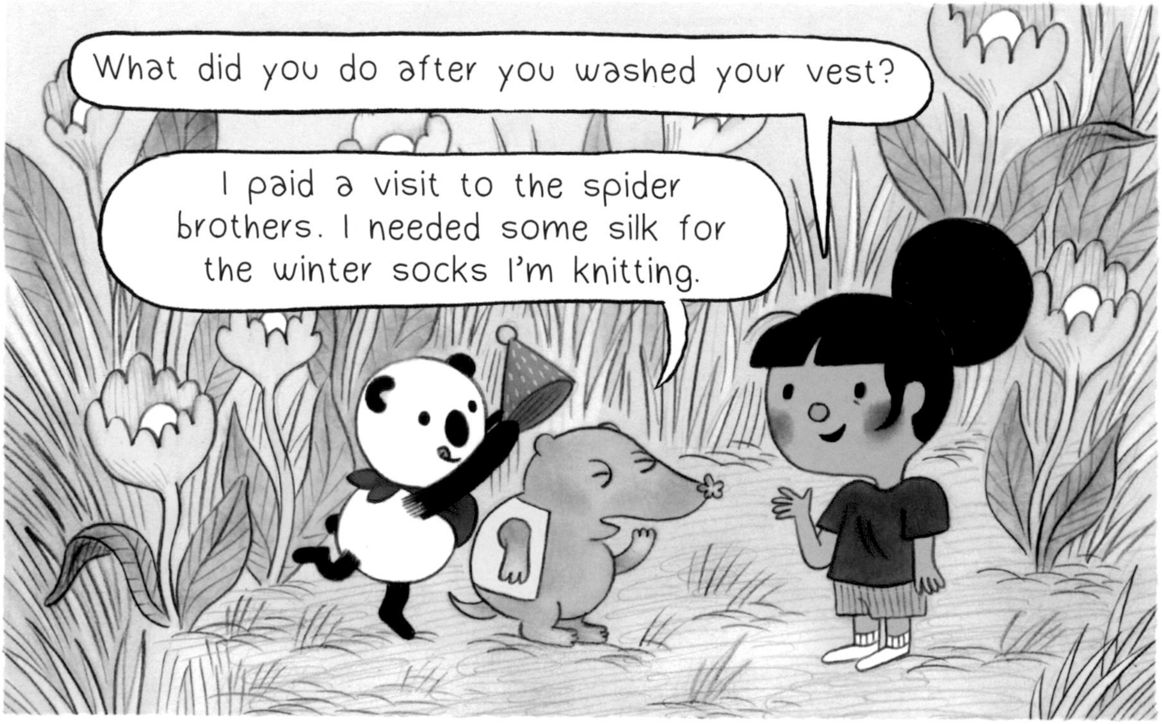
What did you do after you washed your vest?
I paid a visit to the spider brothers. I needed some silk for the winter socks I'm knitting.

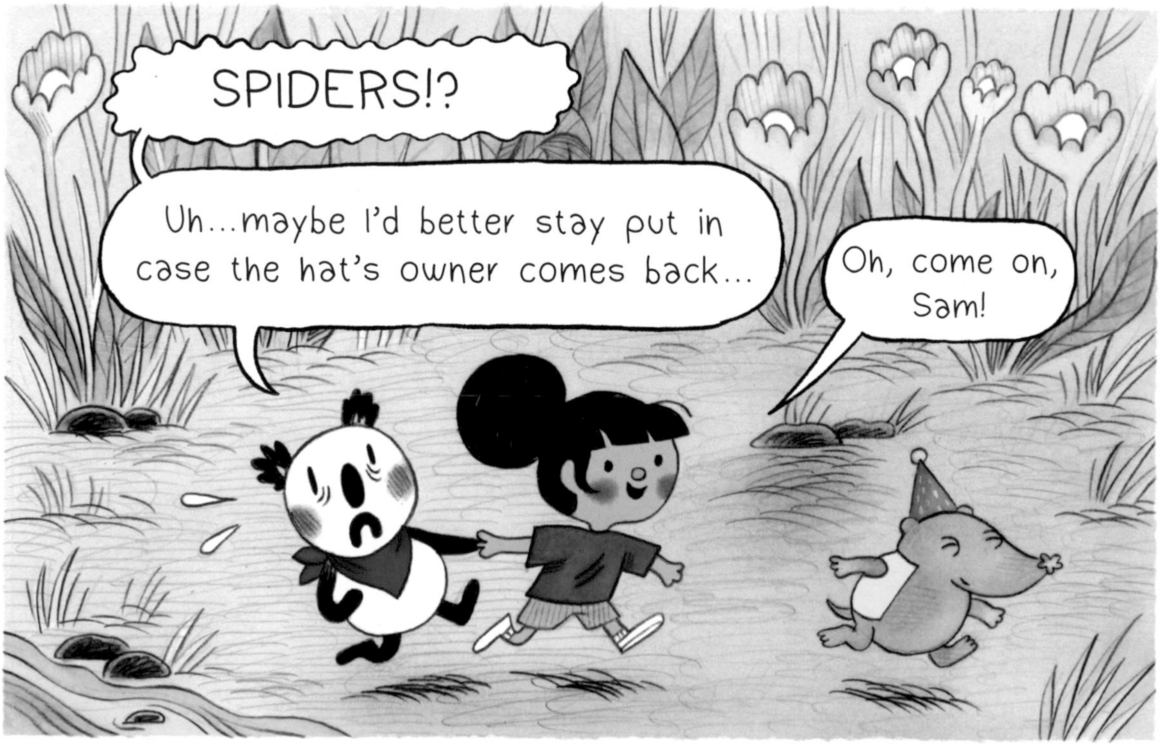
SPIDERS!?
Uh...maybe I'd better stay put in case the hat's owner comes back...
Oh, come on, Sam!

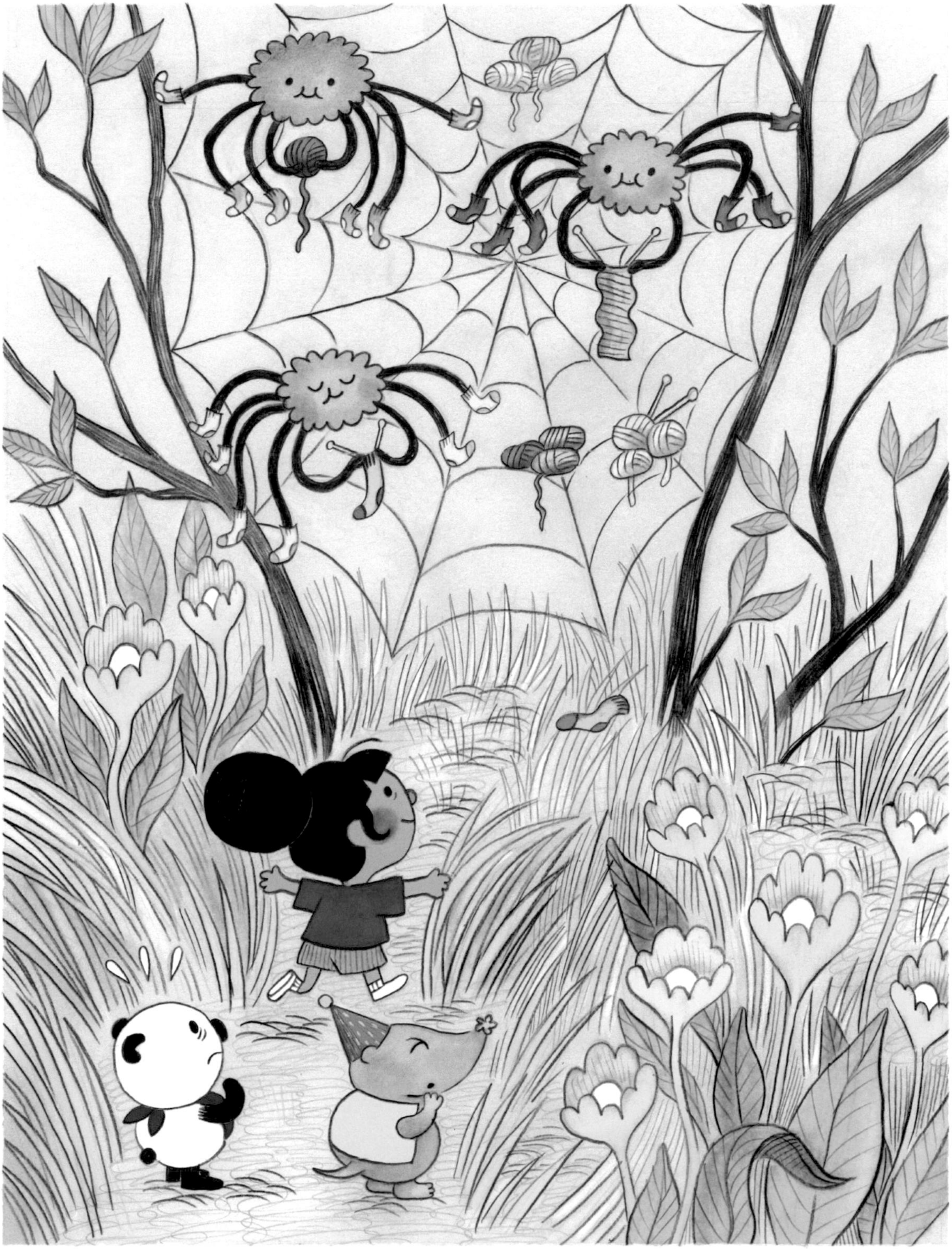

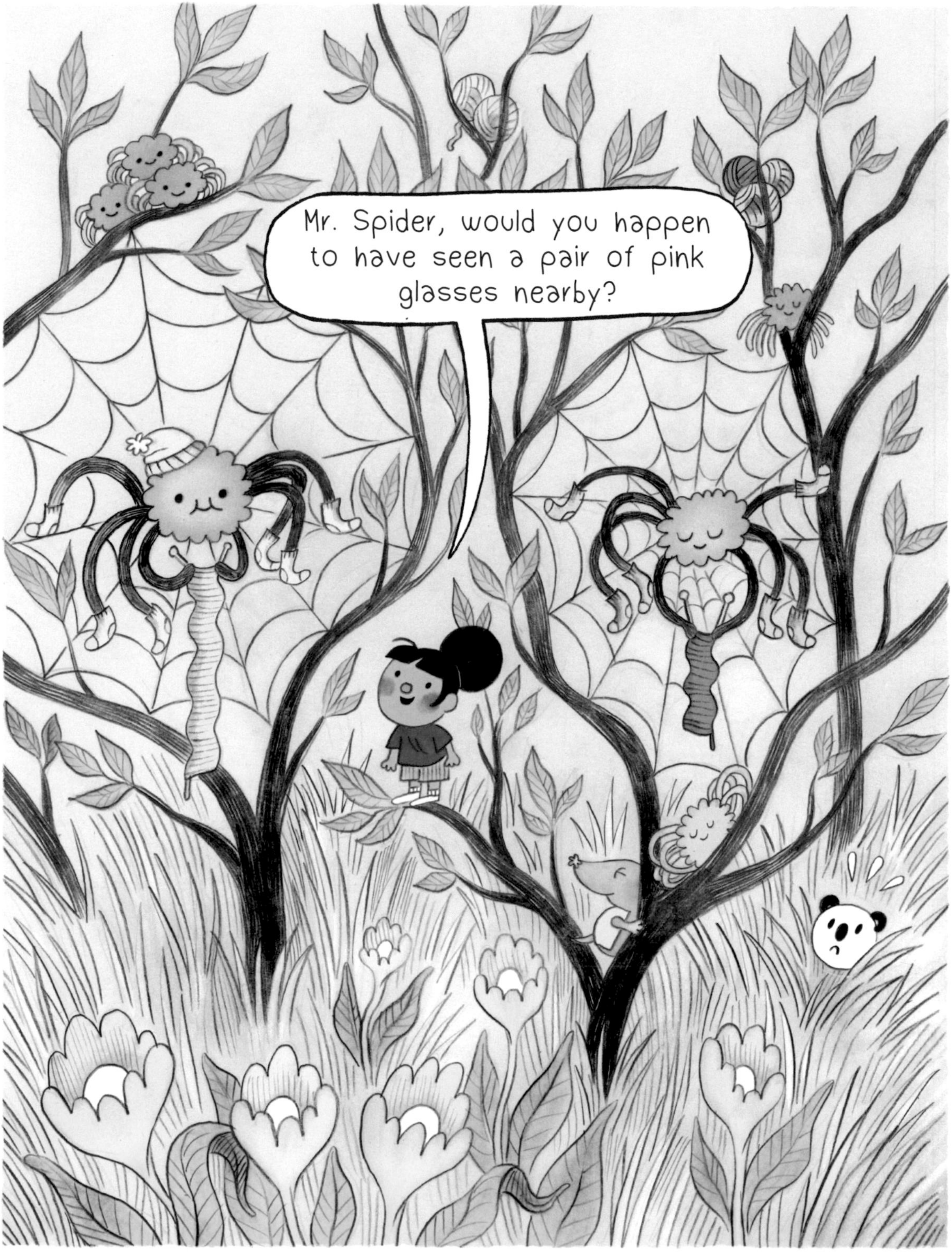
Mr. Spider, would you happen to have seen a pair of pink glasses nearby?

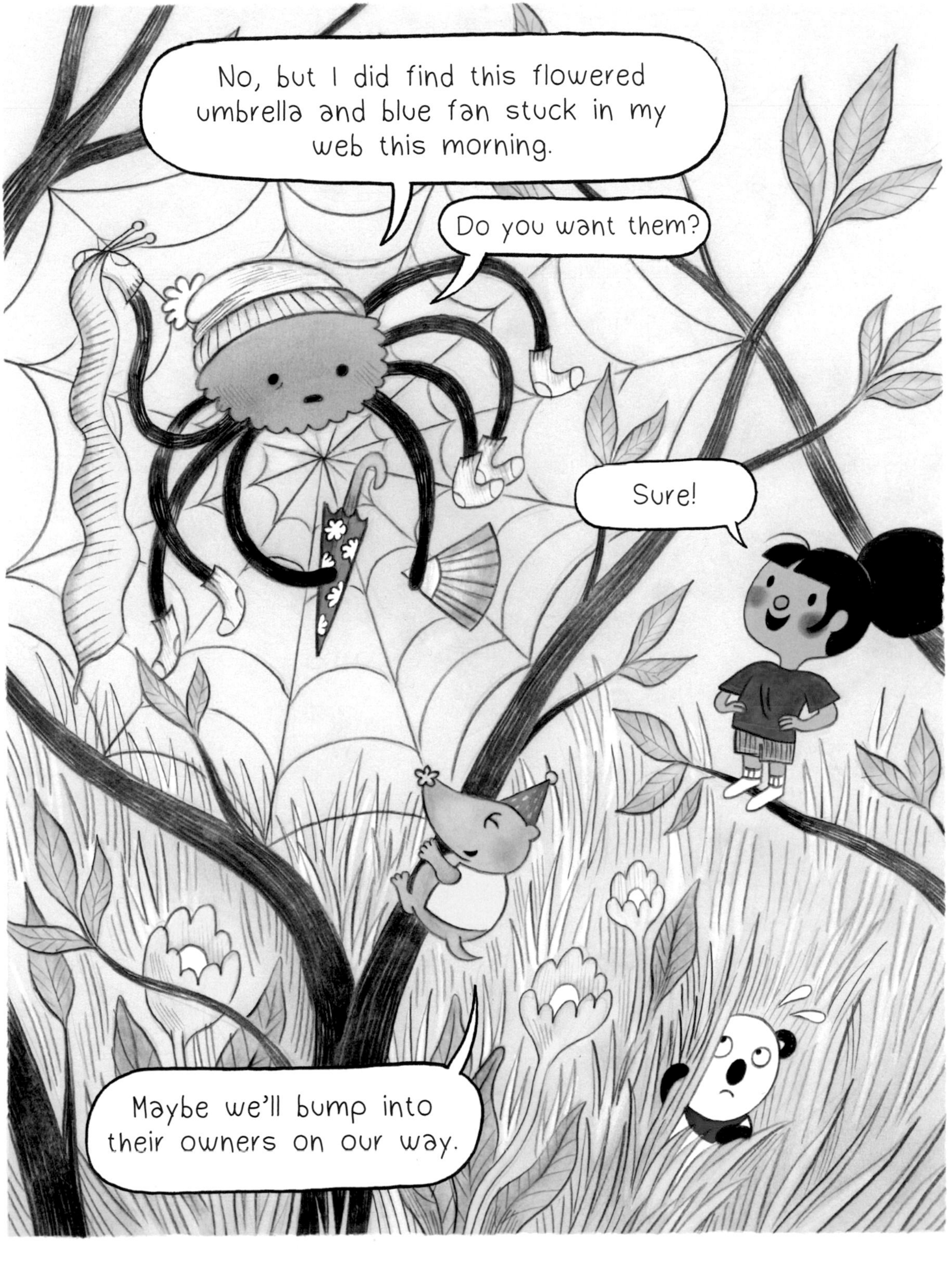
No, but I did find this flowered umbrella and blue fan stuck in my web this morning.
Do you want them?
Sure!
Maybe we'll bump into their owners on our way.

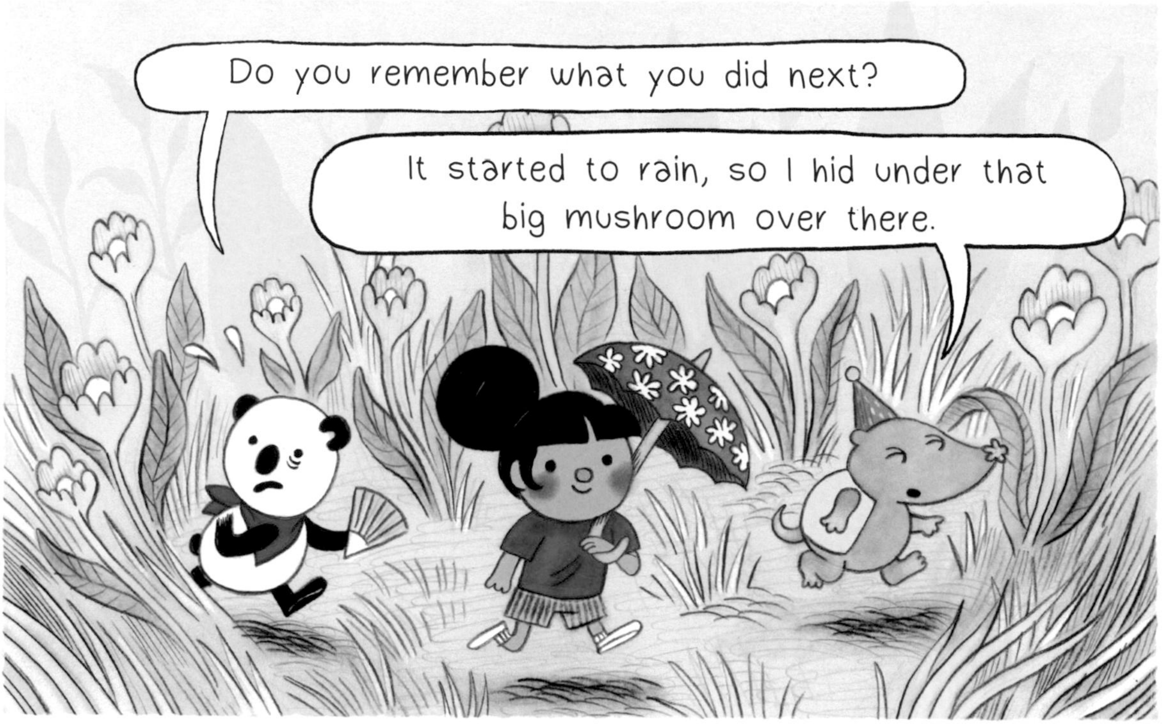
Do you remember what you did next?
It started to rain, so I hid under that big mushroom over there.

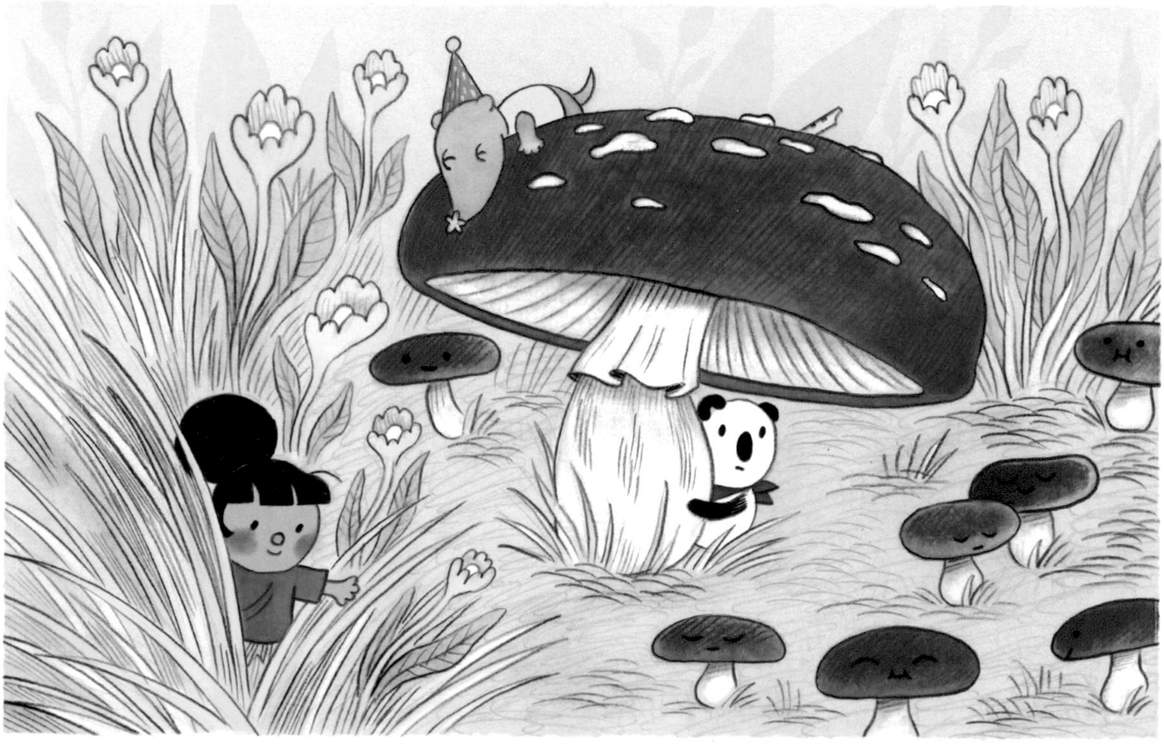

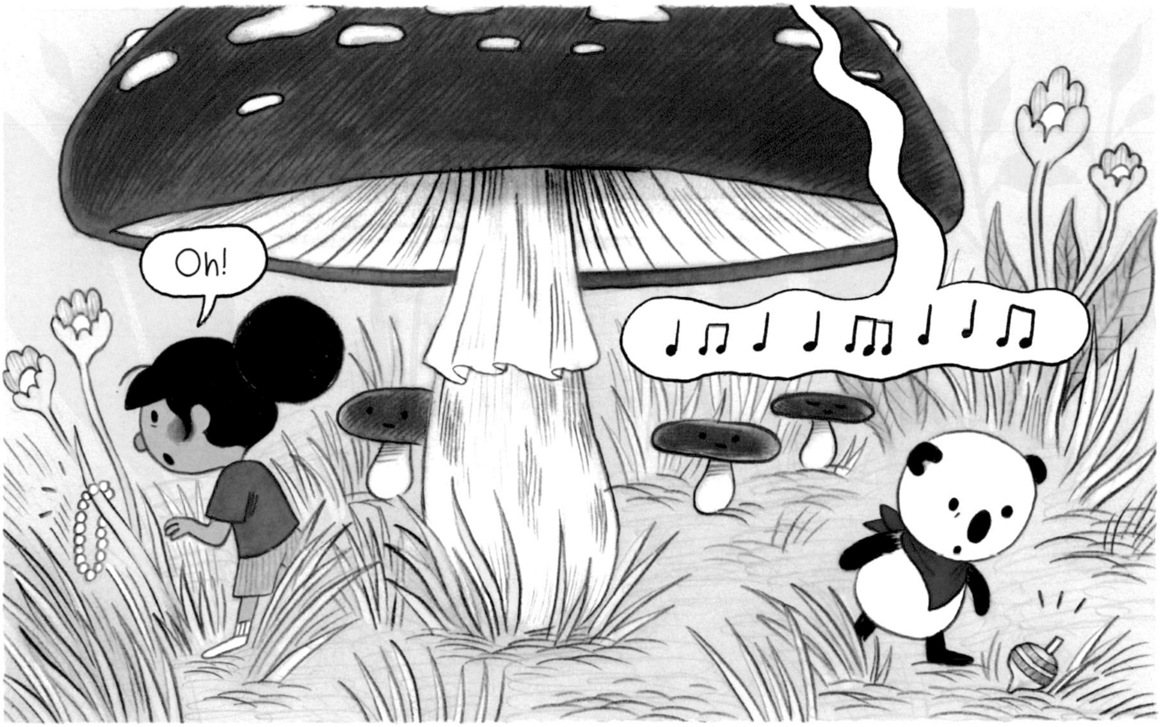
Oh!

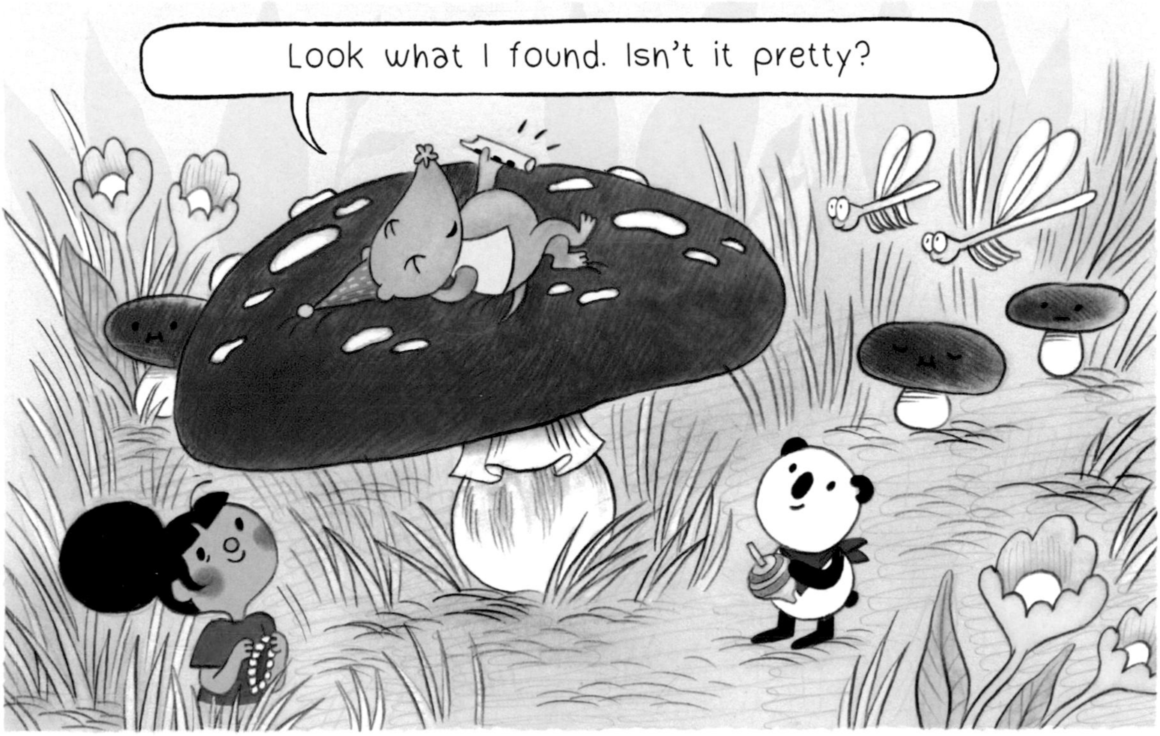
Look what I found. Isn't it pretty?

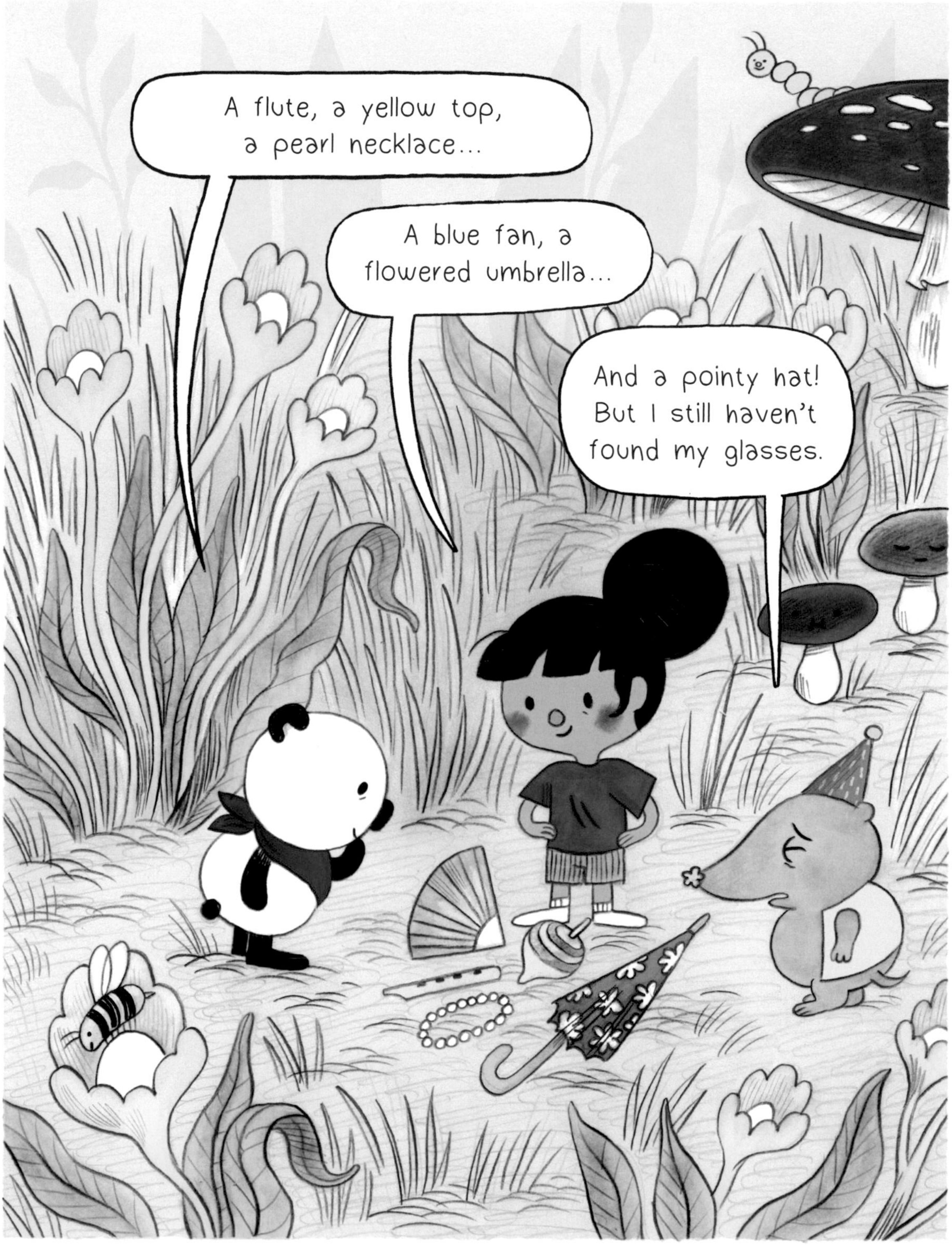
A flute, a yellow top, a pearl necklace...
A blue fan, a flowered umbrella...
And a pointy hat! But I still haven't found my glasses.

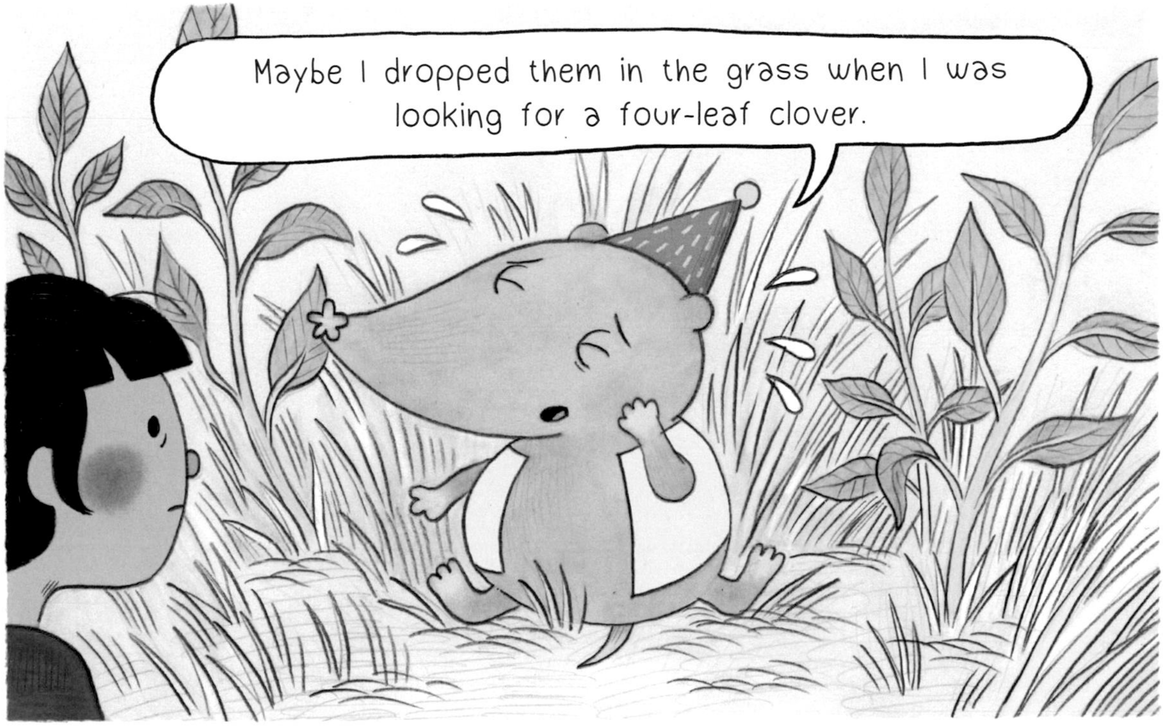
Maybe I dropped them in the grass when I was looking for a four-leaf clover.

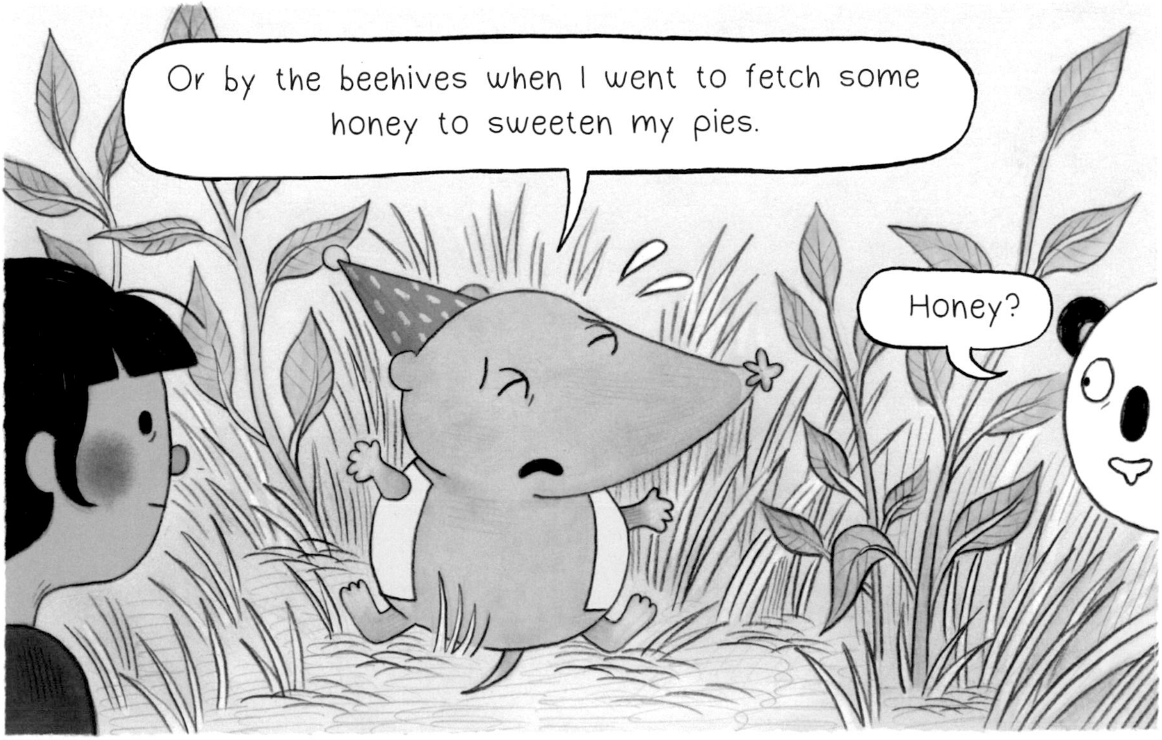
Or by the beehives when I went to fetch some honey to sweeten my pies.
Honey?

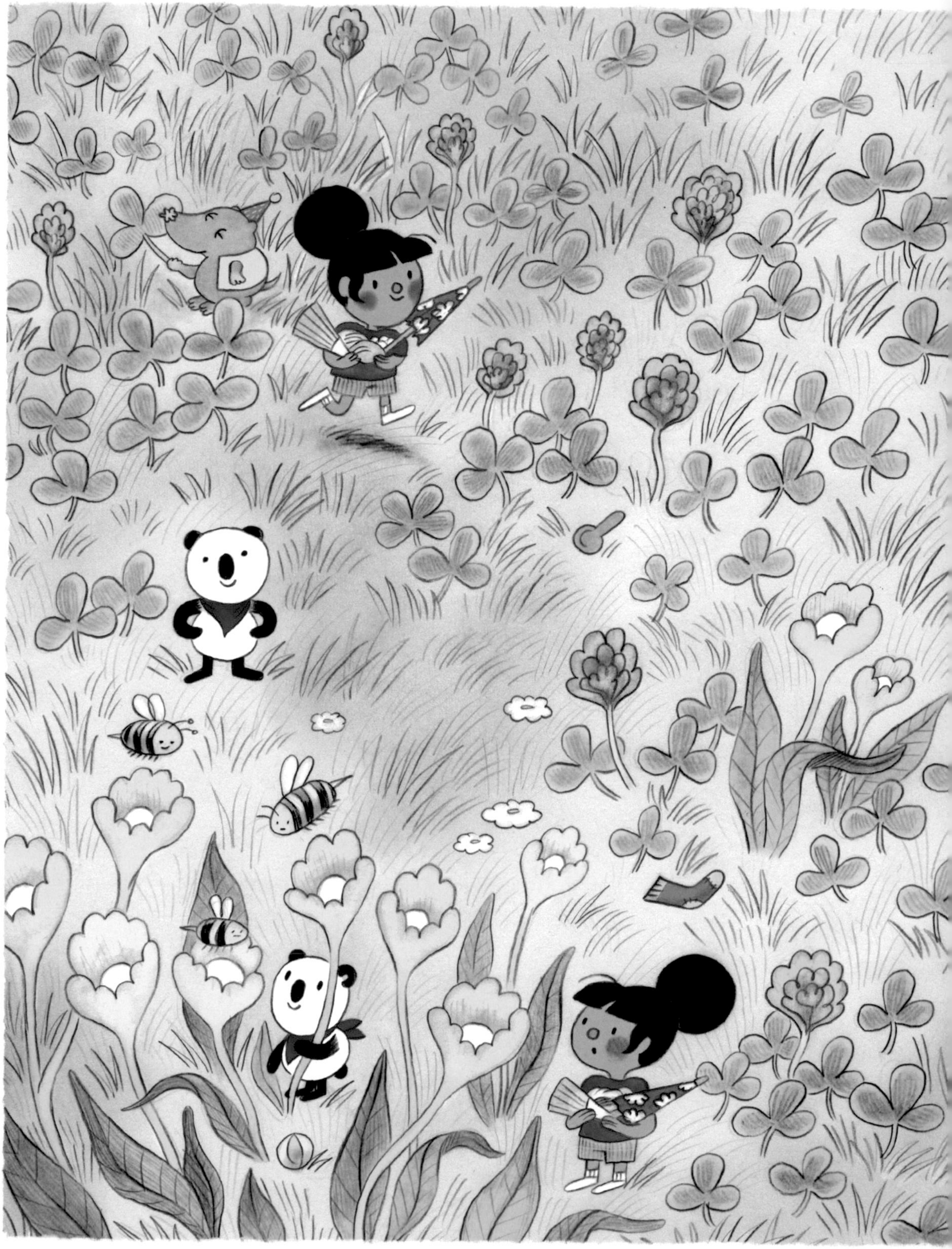

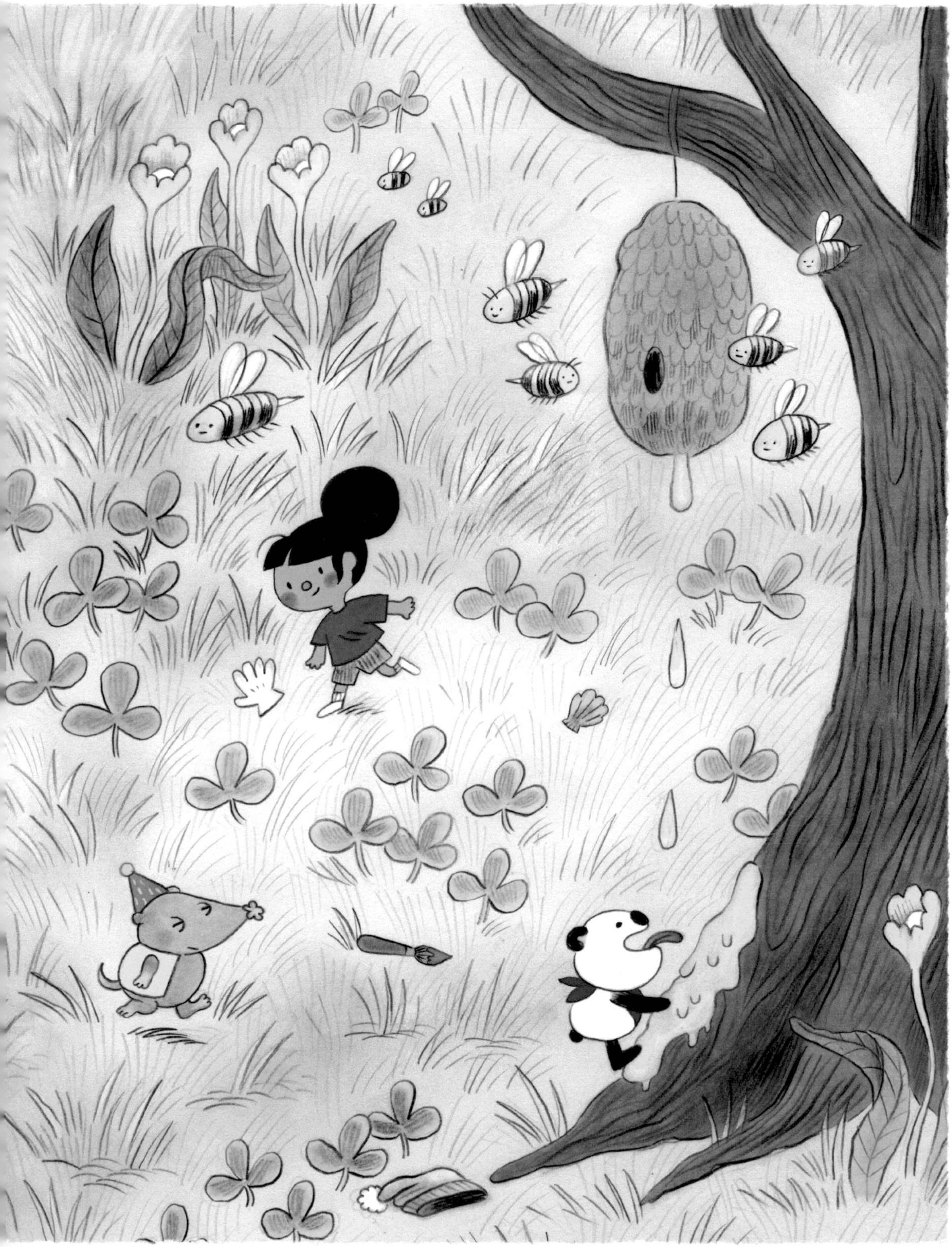

Two hours later...

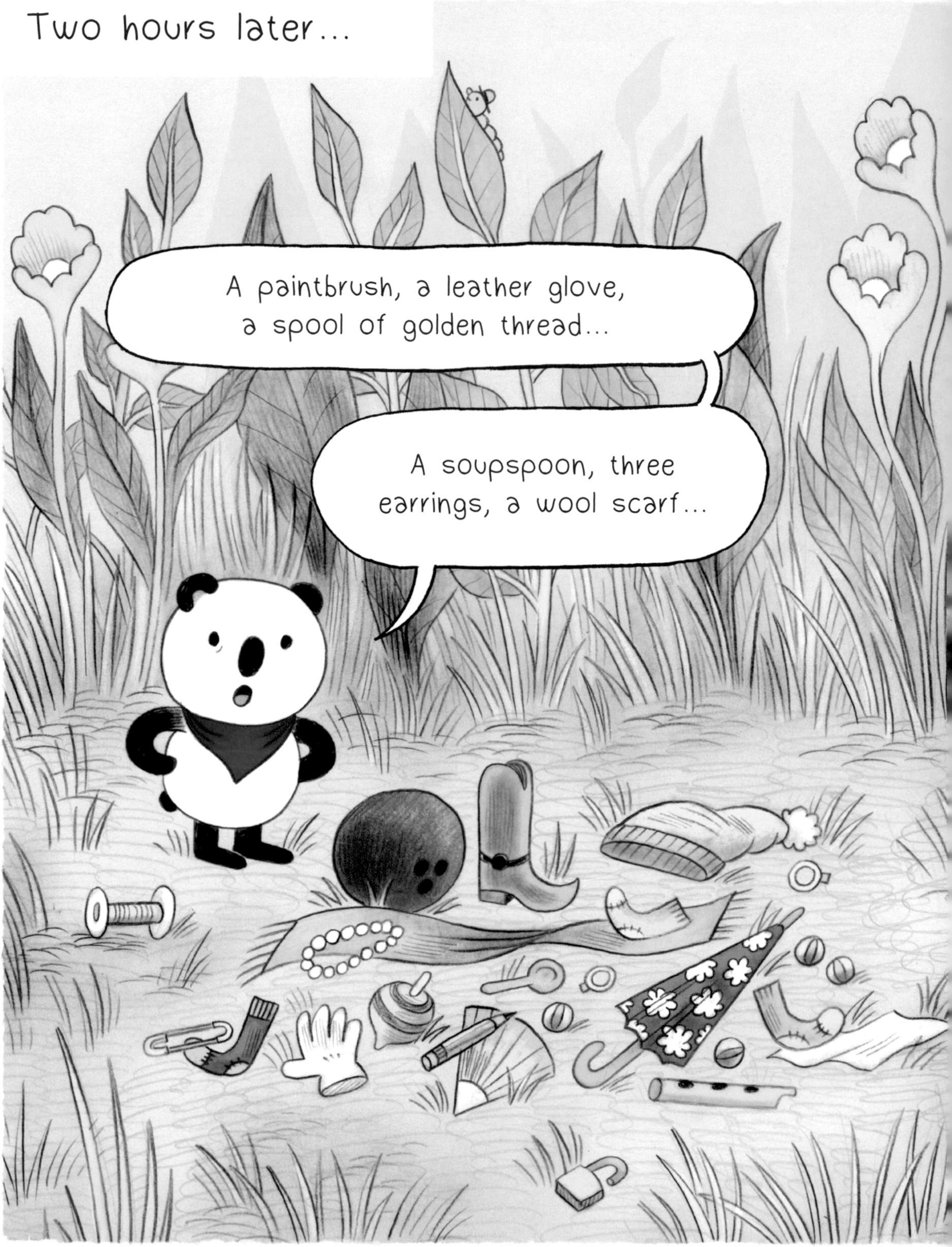
A paintbrush, a leather glove, a spool of golden thread...
A soupspoon, three earrings, a wool scarf...

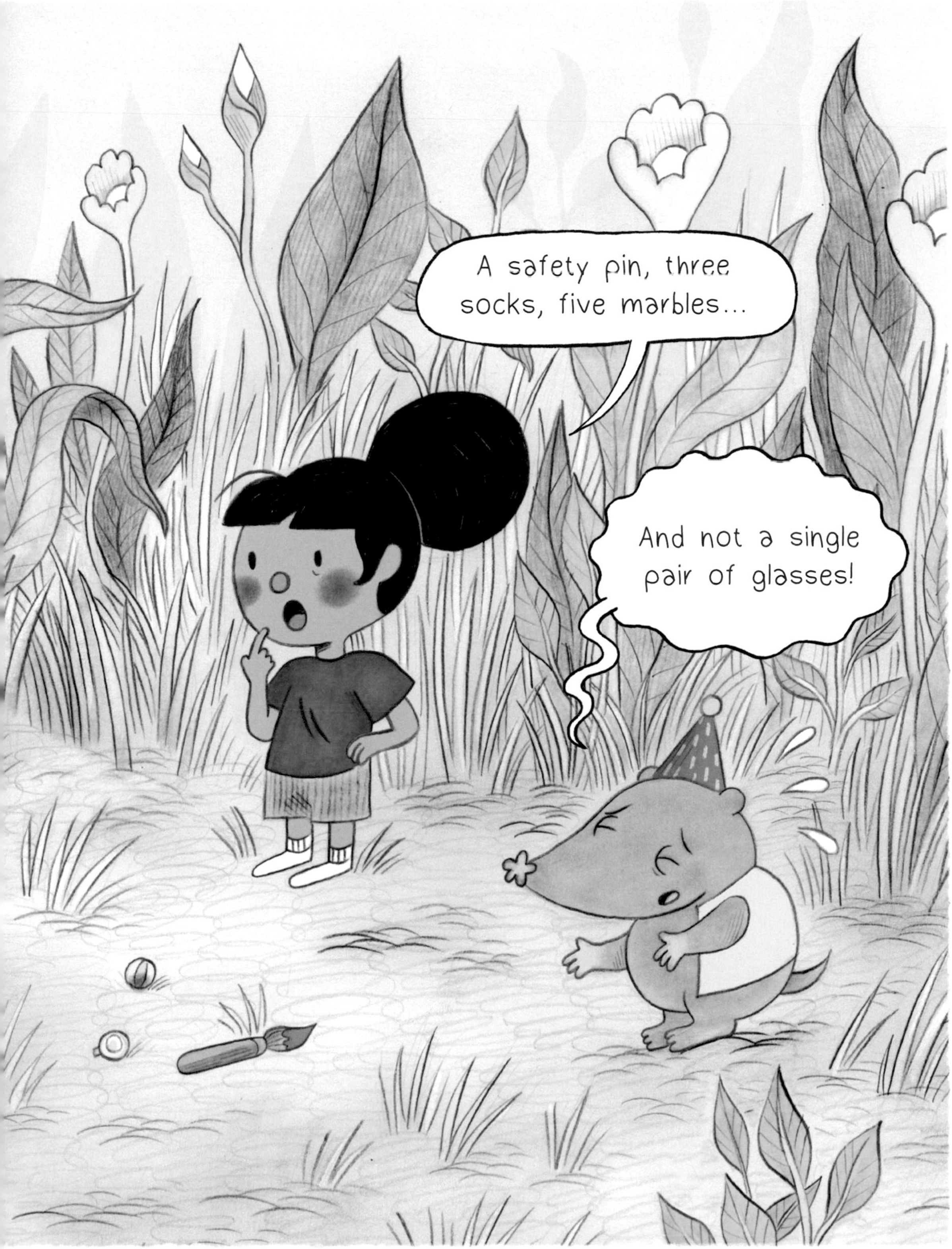
A safety pin, three socks, five marbles...
And not a single pair of glasses!

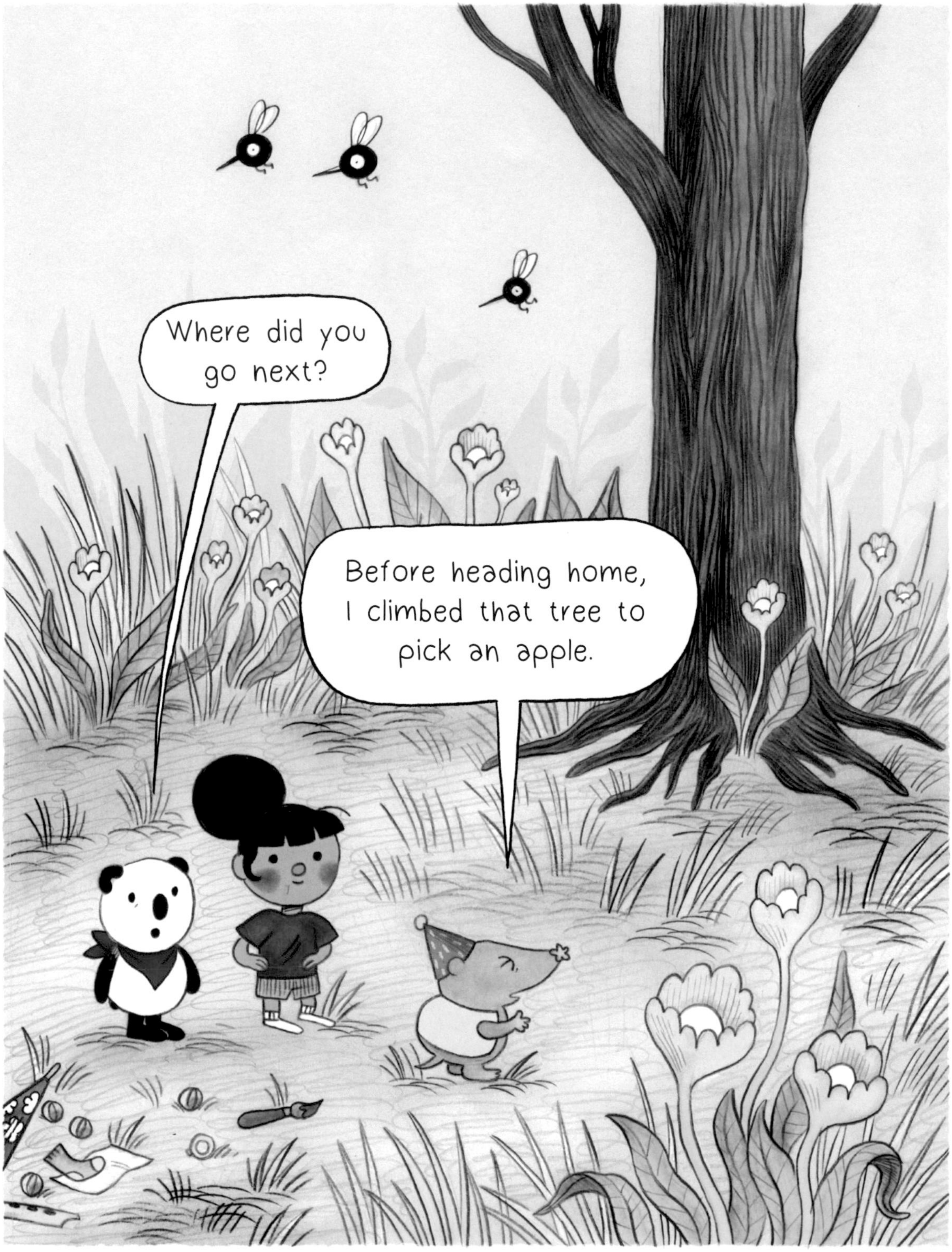
Where did you go next?
Before heading home, I climbed that tree to pick an apple.

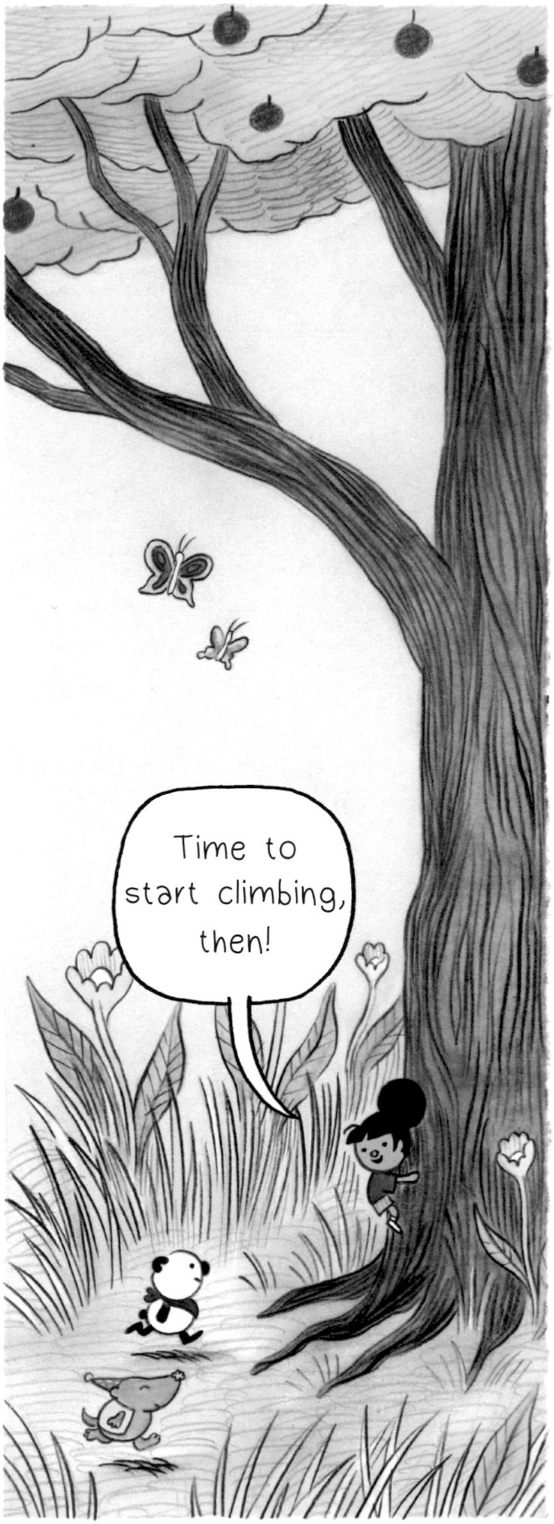
Time to start climbing, then!

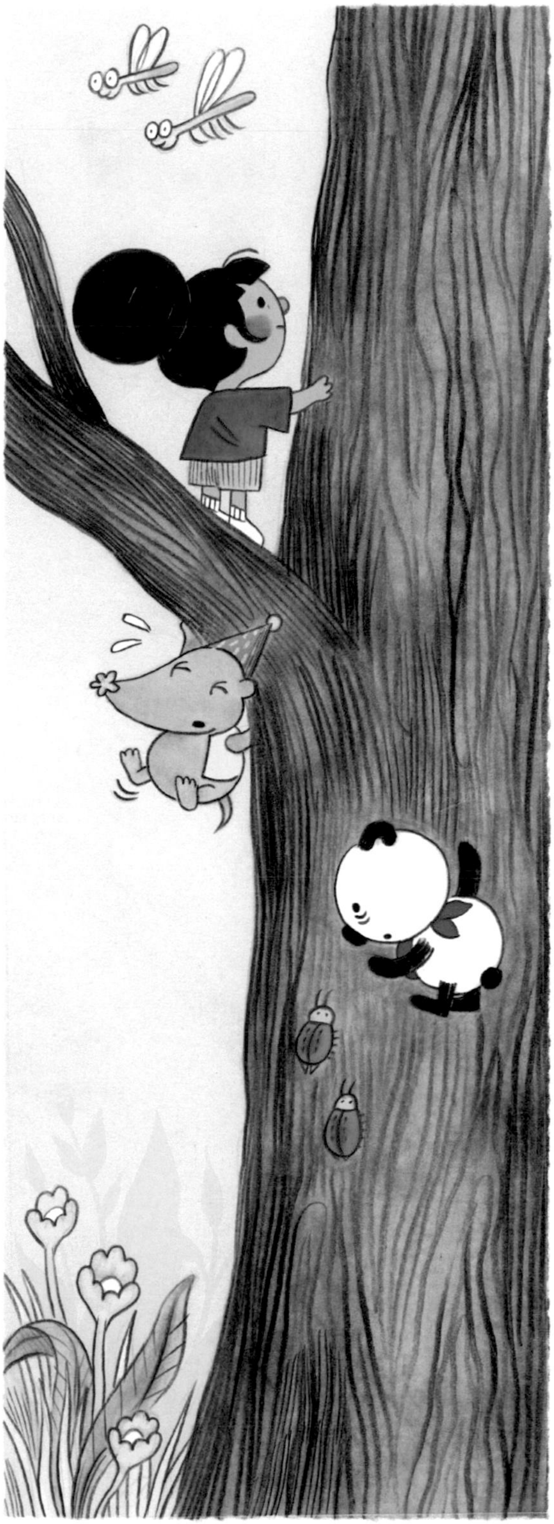

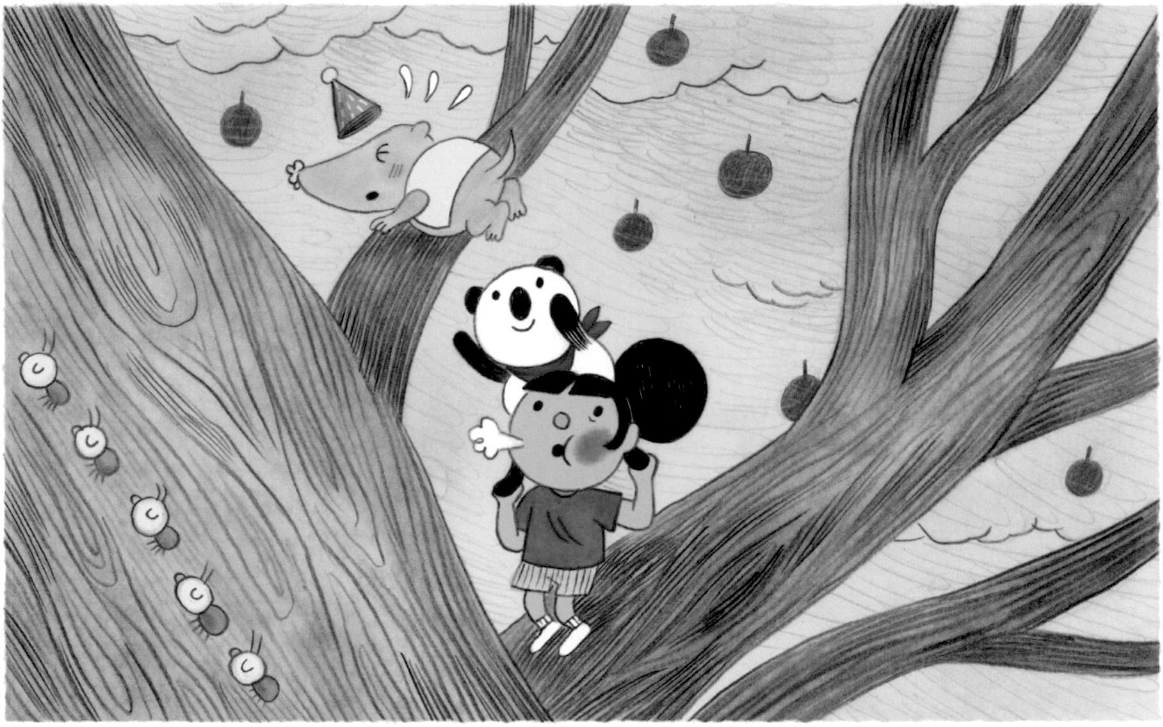

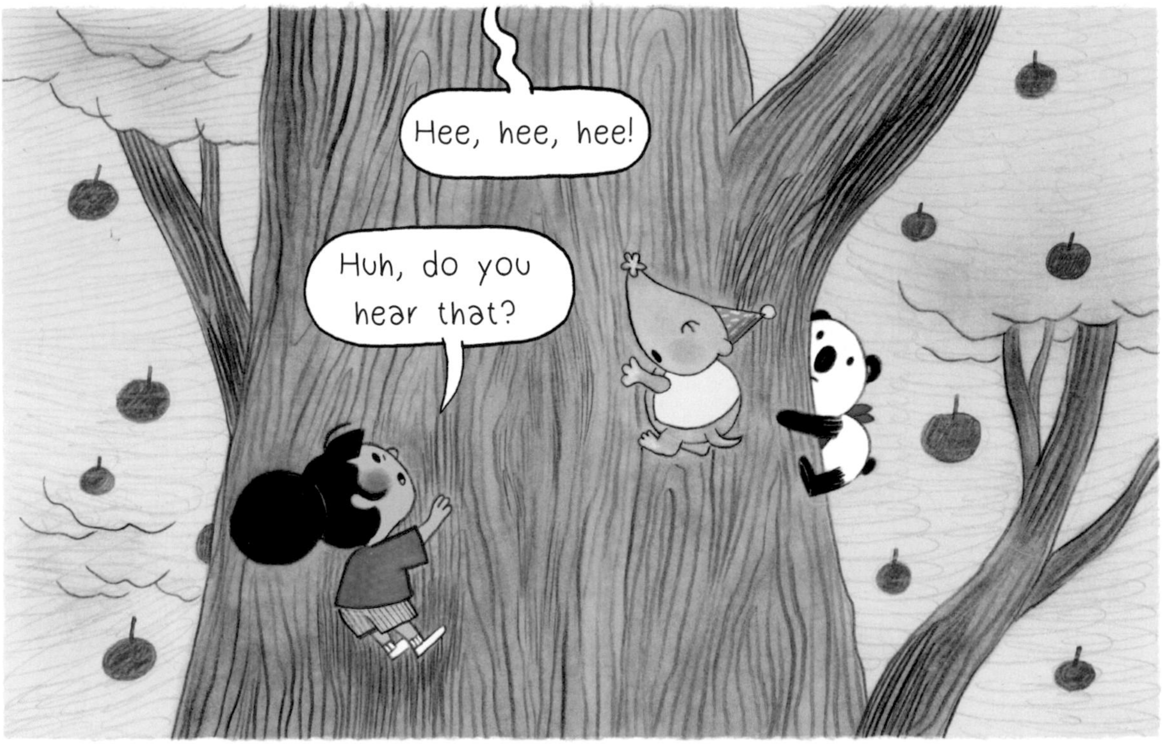
Hee, hee, hee!
Huh, do you hear that?

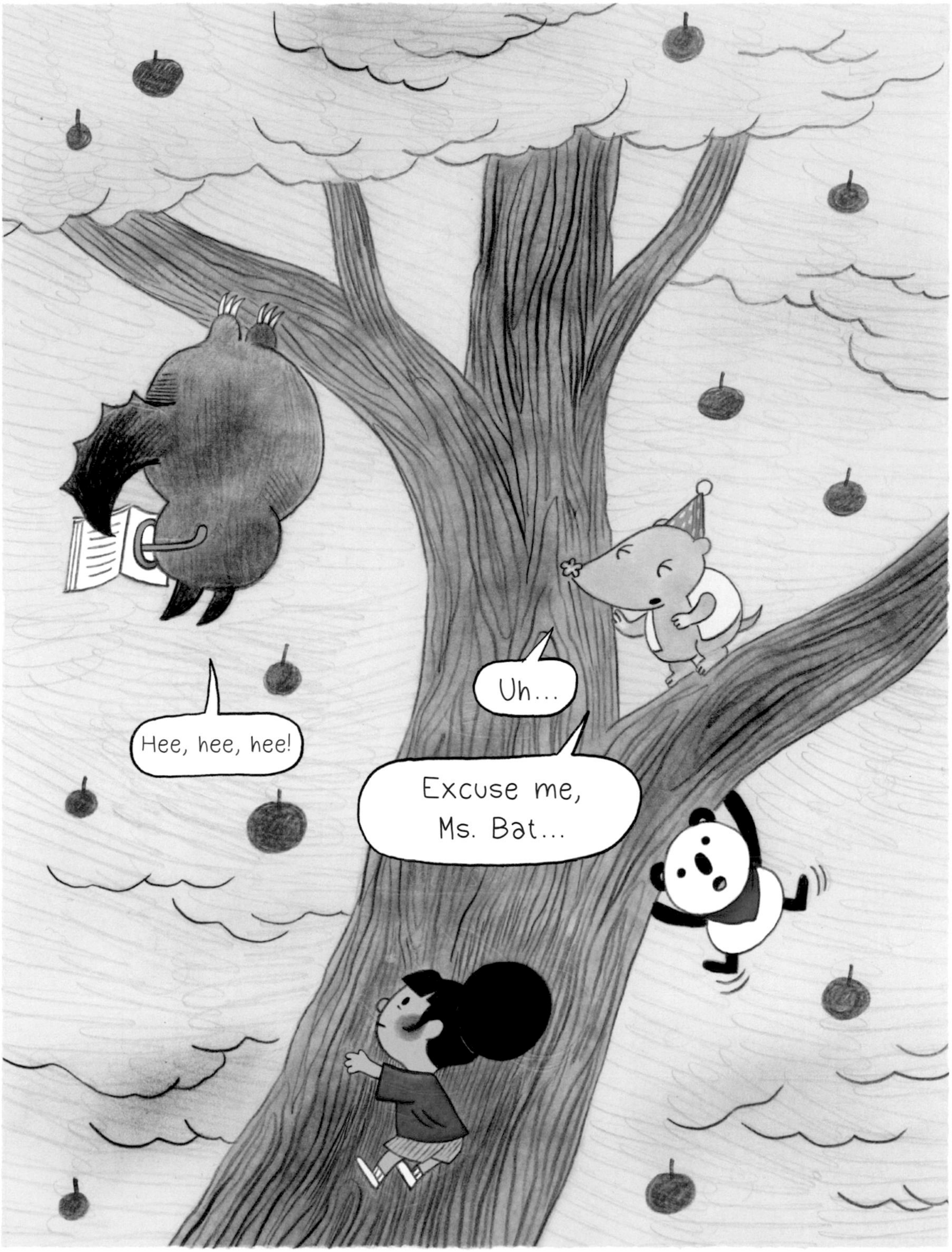
Uh...
Hee, hee, hee!
Excuse me, Ms. Bat...

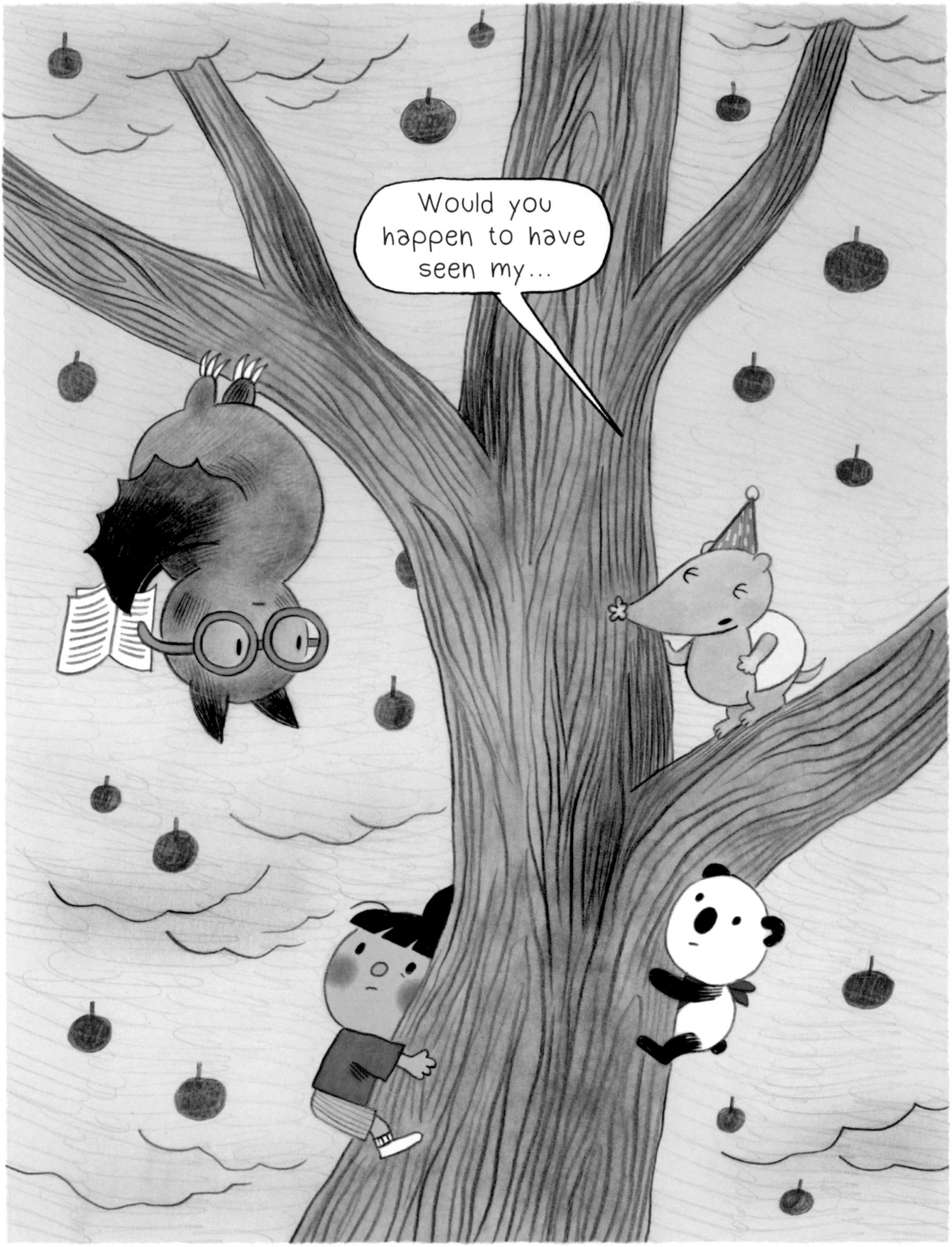
Would you happen to have seen my...

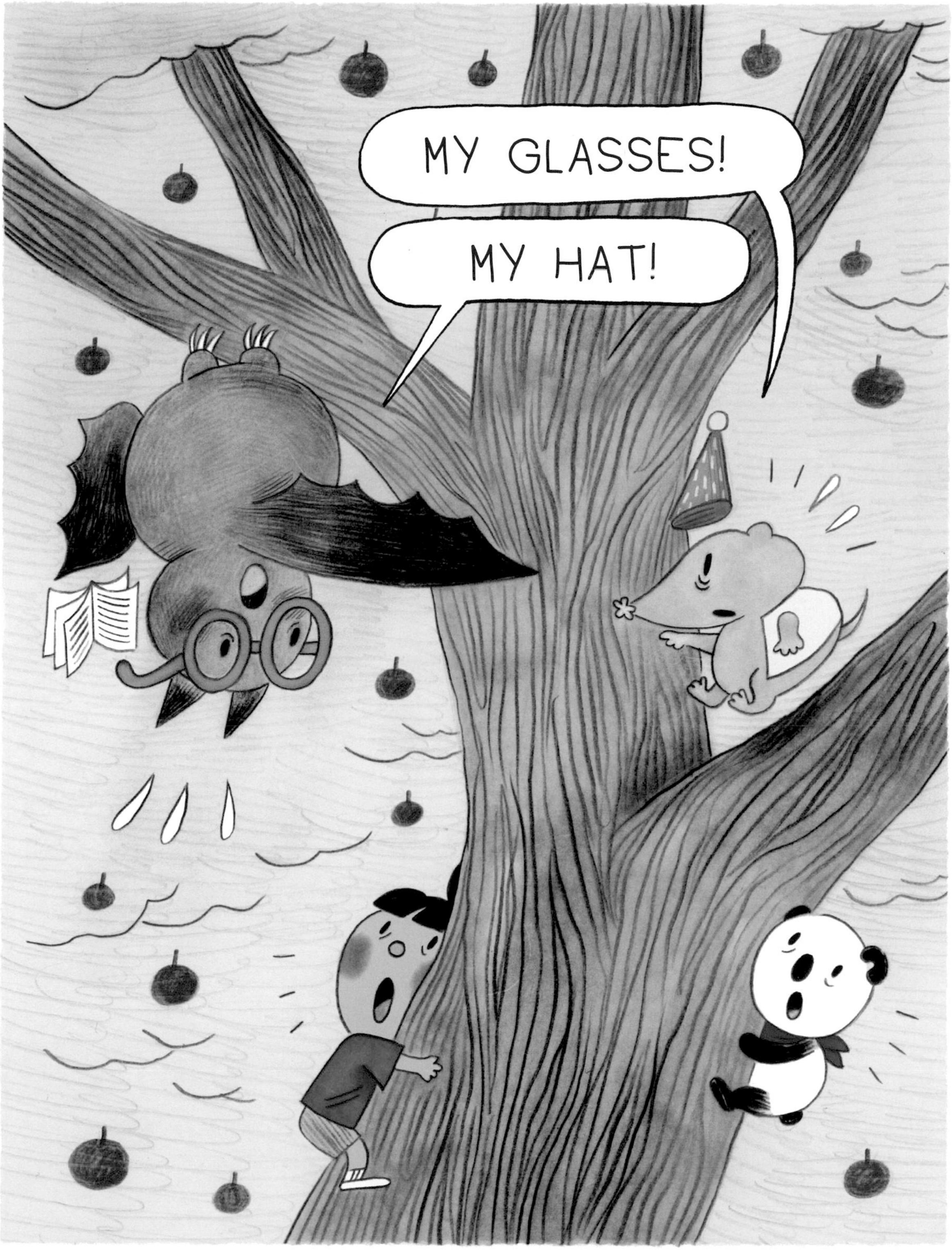
MY GLASSES!
MY HAT!

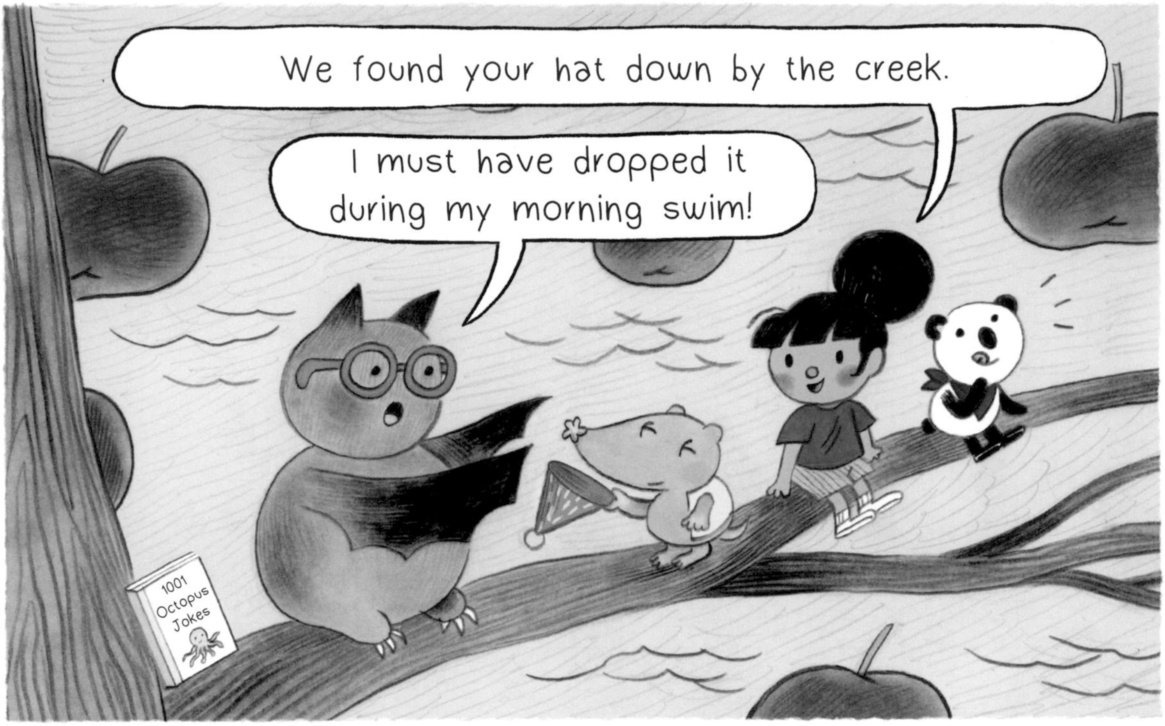
We found your hat down by the creek.
I must have dropped it during my morning swim!
1001 Octopus Jokes

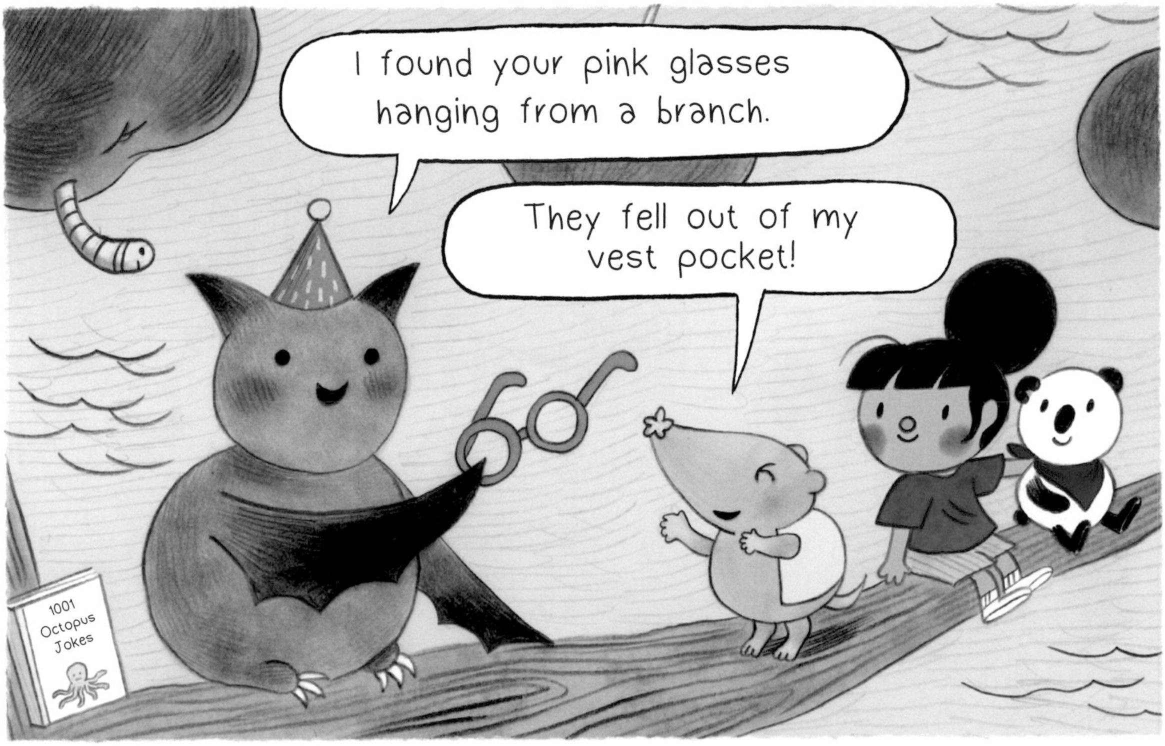
I found your pink glasses hanging from a branch.
They fell out of my vest pocket!
1001 Octopus Jokes

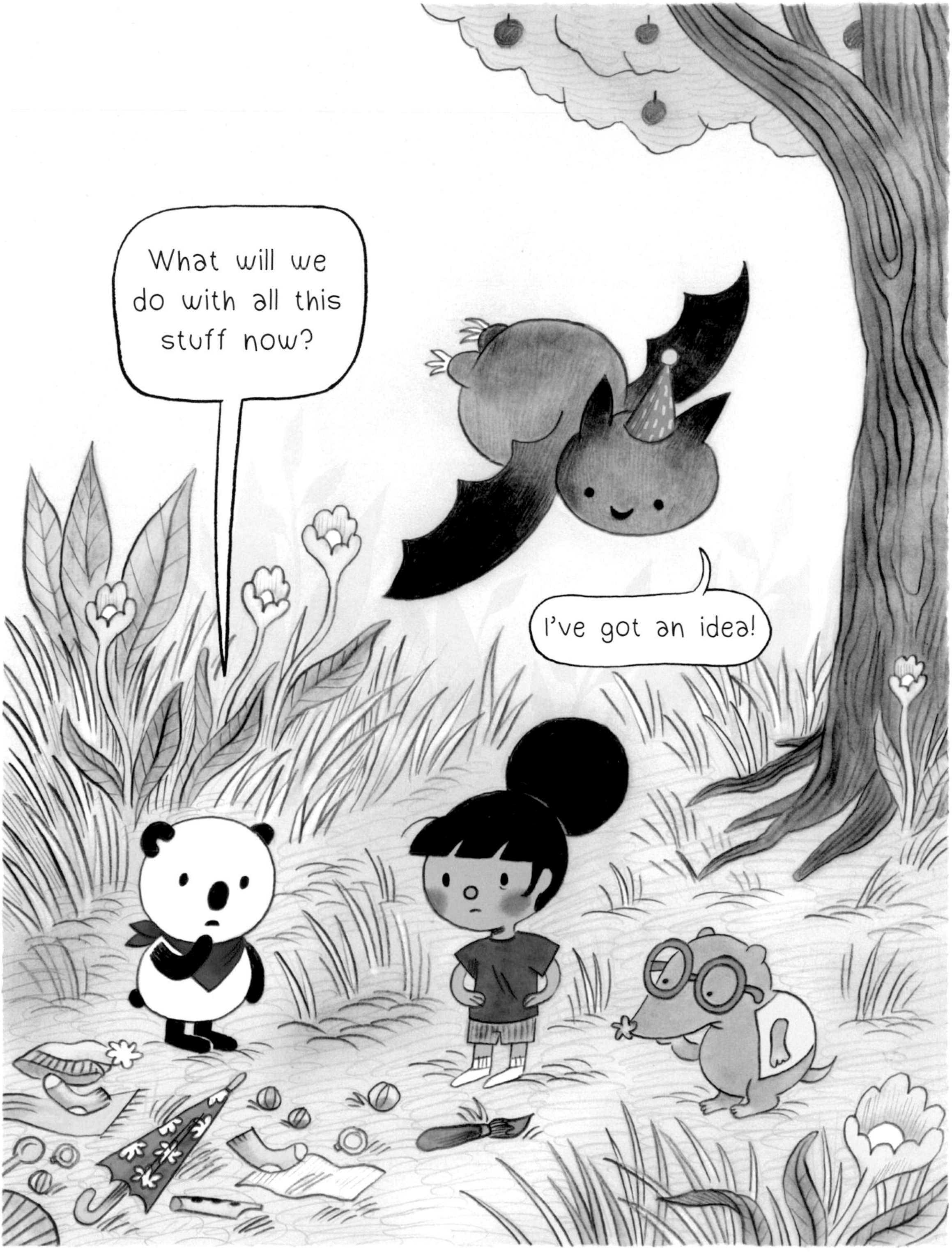
What will we do with all this stuff now?
I've got an idea!

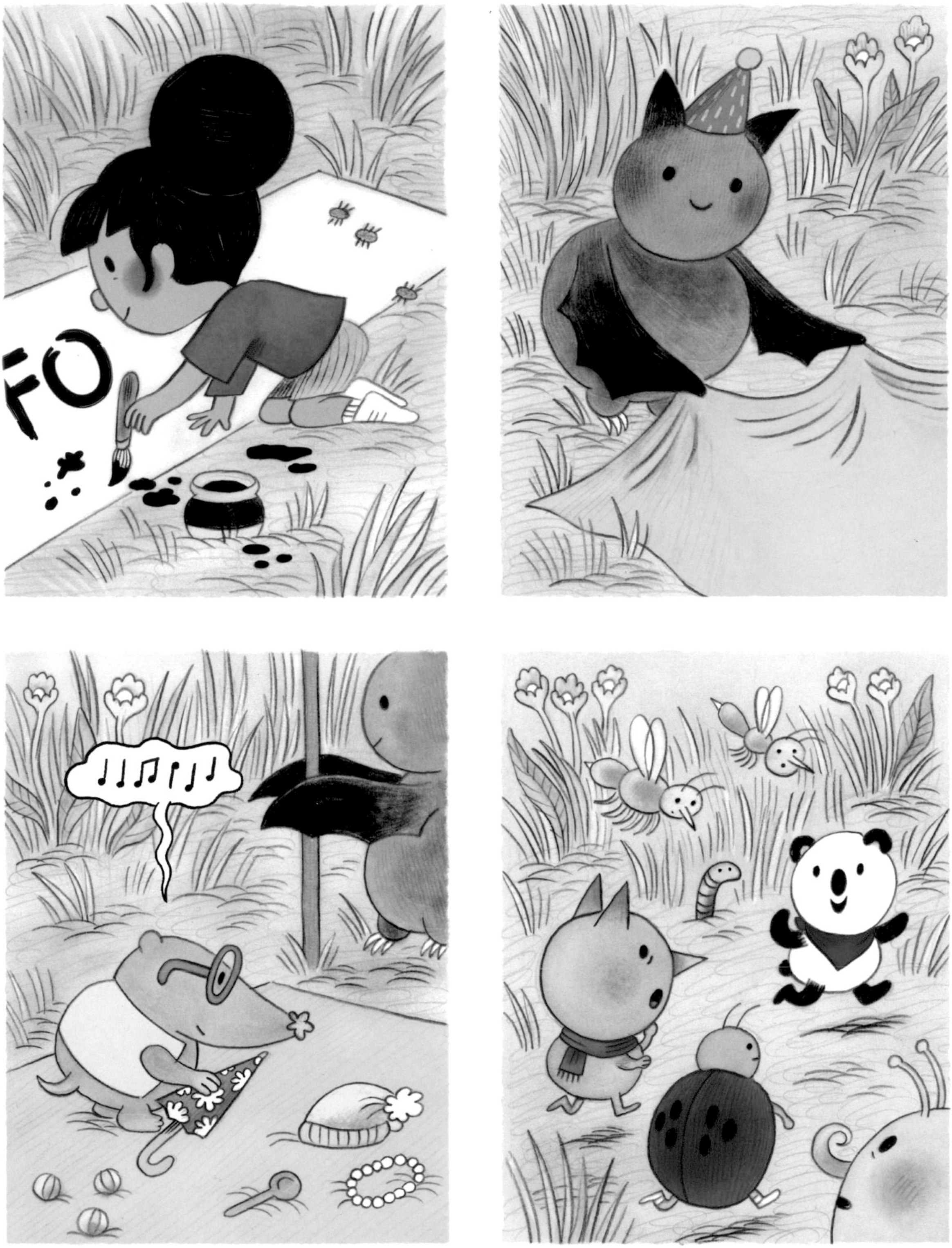
FO

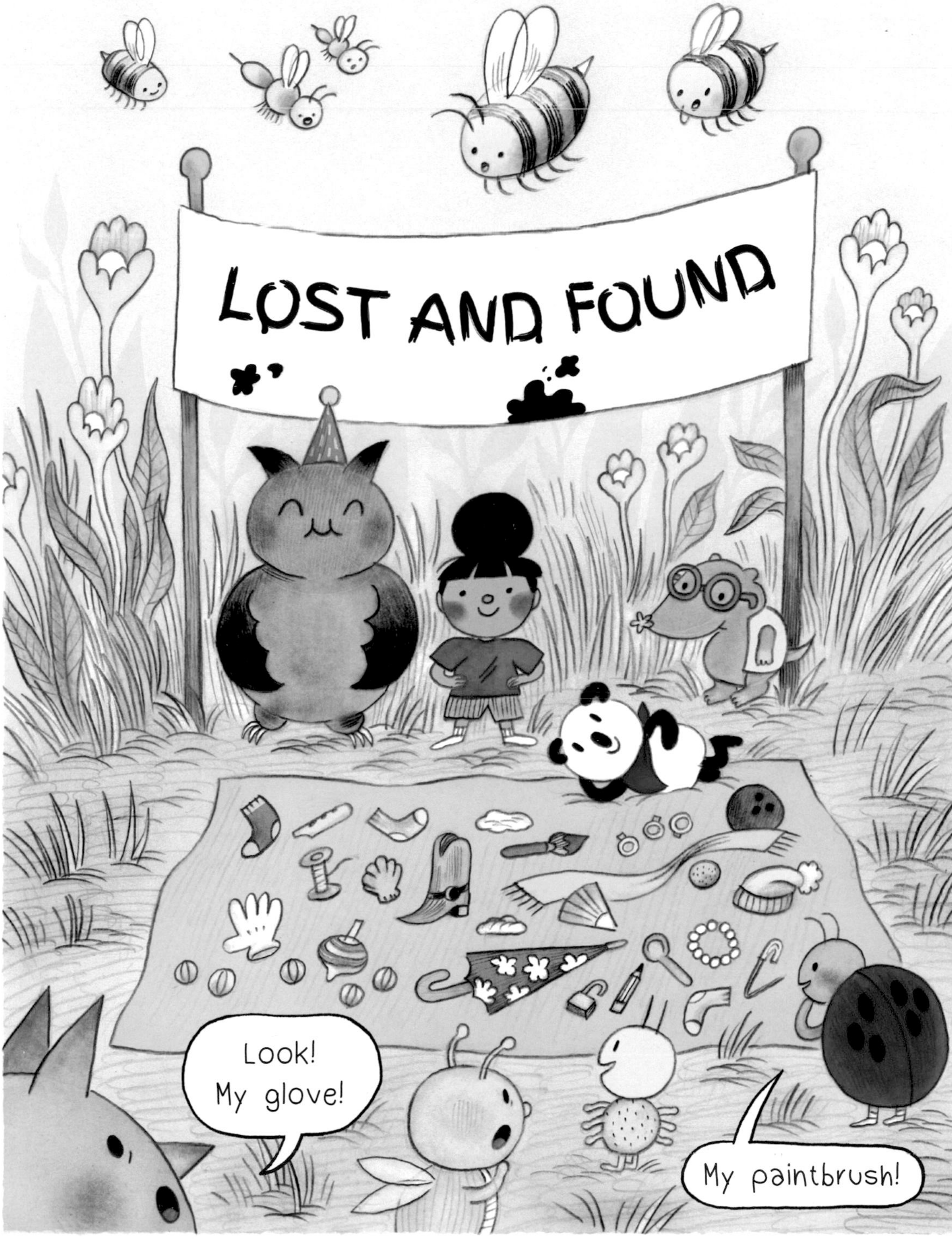
LOST AND FOUND
Look! My glove!
My paintbrush!

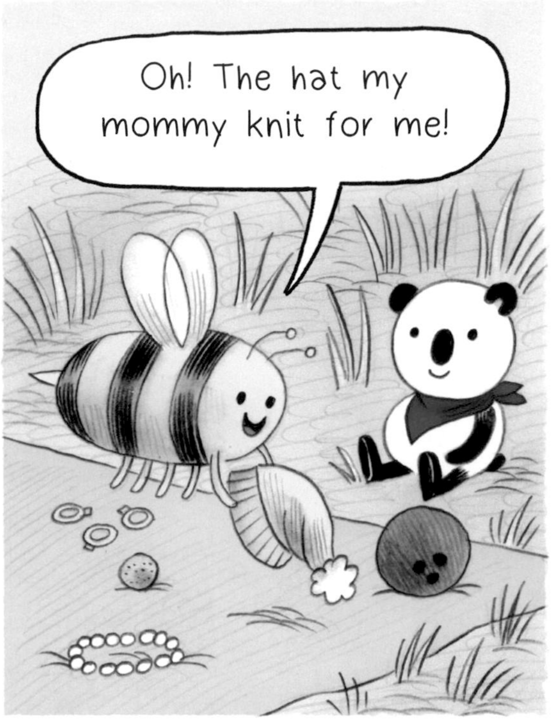
Oh! The hat my mommy knit for me!

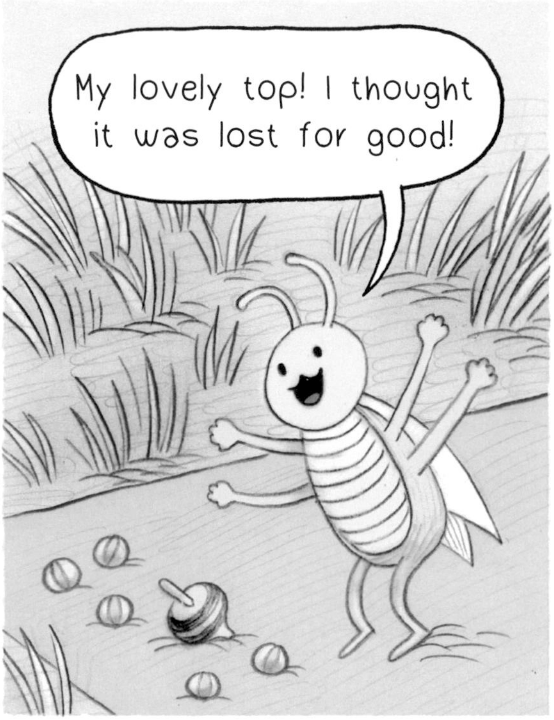
My lovely top! I thought it was lost for good!

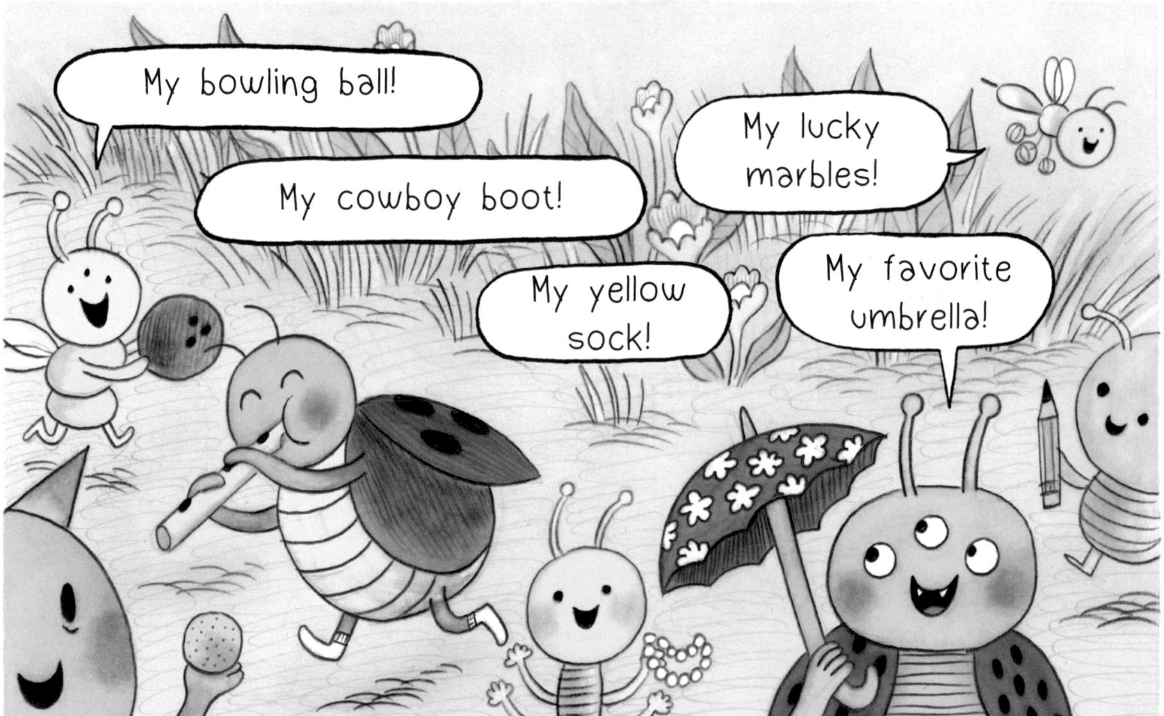
My bowling ball!
My cowboy boot!
My lucky marbles!
My yellow sock!
My favorite umbrella!

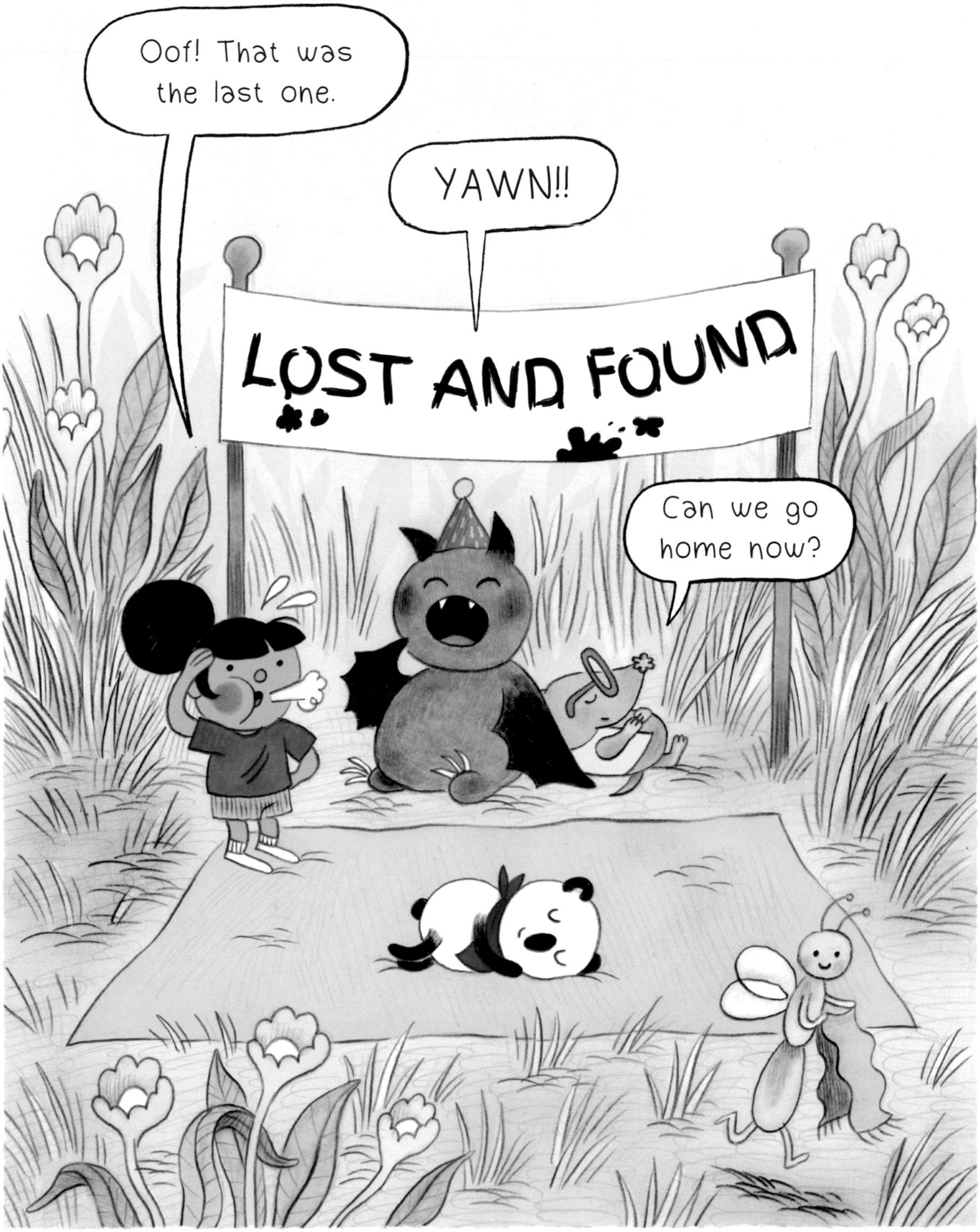
Oof! That was the last one.
YAWN!!
LOST AND FOUND
Can we go home now?

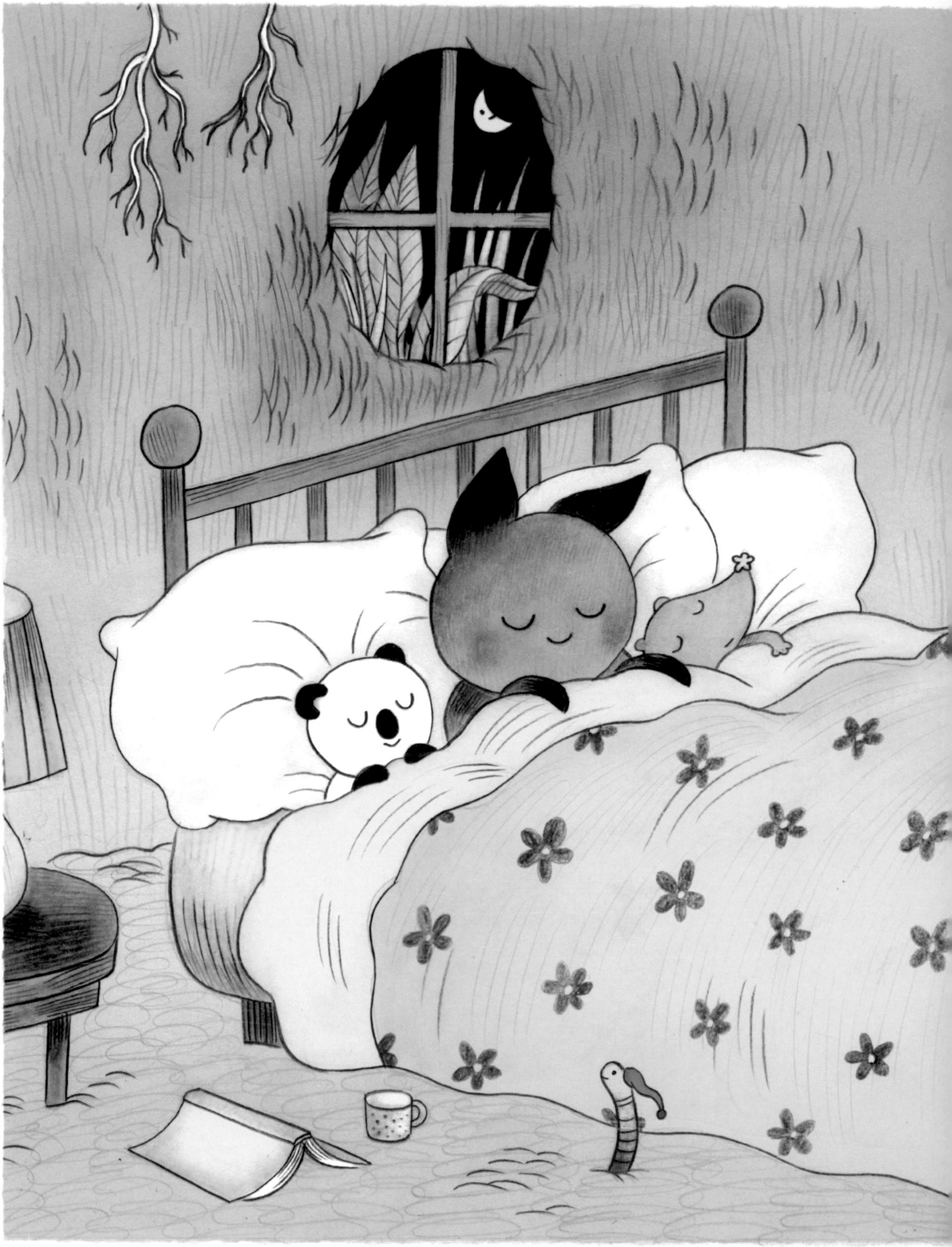

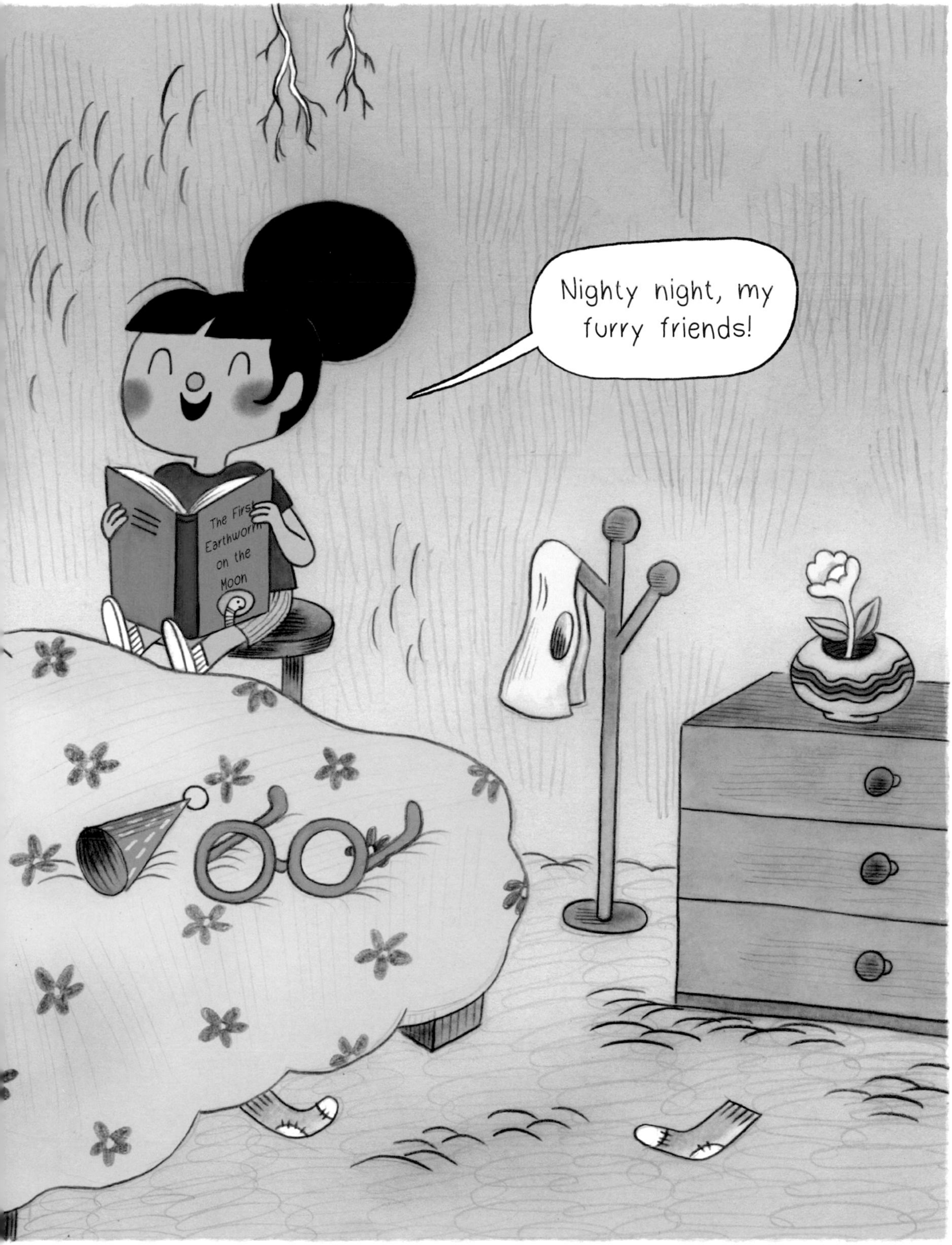
Nighty night, my furry friends!
The First Earthworm on the Moon

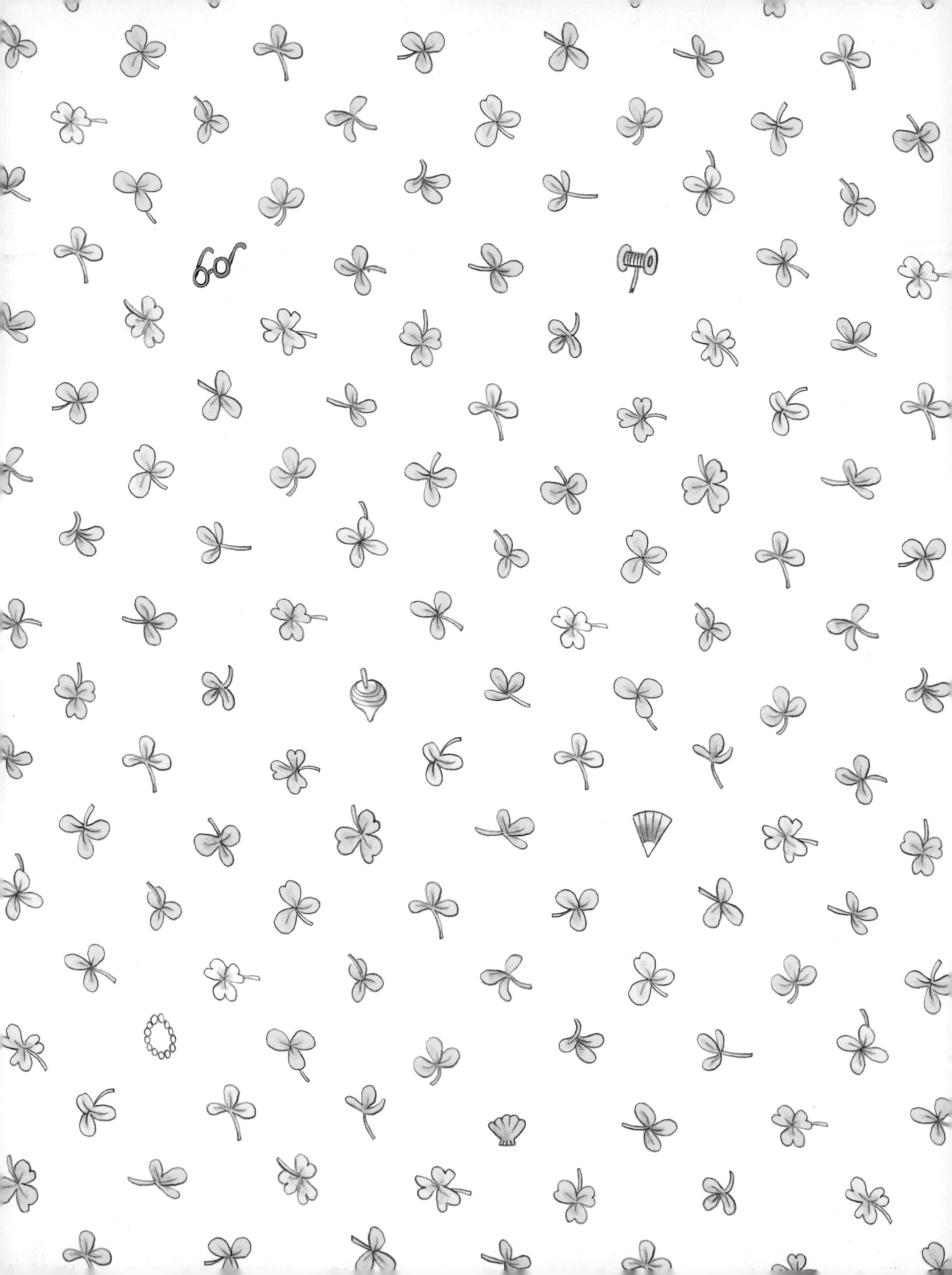